Love's Redemption

Love's Redemption

ShaRhonda L. Sharp

SLS Publishing, LLC

Dear Love,

"Love is patient and kind; love does not envy or boast; it is not arrogant or rude. It does not insist on its own way; it is not irritable or resentful; it does not rejoice at wrongdoing, but rejoices with the truth. Love bears all things, believes all things, hopes all things, endures all things."
1 Corinthians 13:4-7 (ESV)

Contents

Prologue

July - Five Years Ago

The sounds of shuffling papers, pens scribbling across surfaces and confidential whispers all created a muffled chorus around Noelle as she sat in Monroe County courthouse for the last time. Today 'Noelle Angelique Pastor' returns to 'Noelle Angelique Morgan.' She had sat in this courtroom more than a dozen times over the last eighteen months petitioning for a divorce from the man she once loved more than air, Eric Pastor.

Noelle peeked around her lawyer's back to steal a glance at her soon-to-be ex-husband. *GOD! He was gorgeous!* So, eloquent, charming, well-mannered and educated. He was a criminal defense attorney in Rochester, New York. At the tender age of twenty-five years old, he already had more successful cases to his credit than most colleagues twice his age. He graduated from New York University Law School with honors, prestige, and multiple job offers at some of the top law firms in the state.

Eric was already well-respected throughout the legal community, a great conversationalist, a fantastic storyteller and a brilliant lawyer. Noelle even had to admit he was a terrific lover. Not that she had much to compare it to – he had been her one and only. Yet, with all the countless accolades acquired over the years, there was one negative mark on his record that overshadowed everything else – Eric Pastor was a lousy husband. No matter how Noelle tried to rationalize his behavior, she just didn't have the heart to forgive, nor the strength to try to make their marriage work. Not anymore.

The judge's booming voice echoing throughout the courtroom made Noelle snap back to the harsh reality that the life she once knew had officially come to an end.

"As requested by the petitioner, Mrs. Noelle Pastor," the judge announced. "She will be granted all personal assets listed in her name and any profits gained from the selling of the condo shared with Mr. Pastor. Mrs. Pastor is not seeking any alimony or spousal support. So, Mr. Pastor is free to keep all monetary assets acquired throughout the course of their marriage. Mrs. Pastor, I wish you the best of luck on all future endeavors. Court adjourned."

With a ceremonious bang of his gavel, it became official. Noelle was now a single woman once again. The marriage she had prided herself on was now over. As she stood to leave, she saw Eric making his way over to her. Noelle braced herself as he approached, not sure what to expect. Eric flashed his thousand-watt smile that melted the hearts of many women – there was a time when she had been one of them.

"Well, Noelle," Eric began. "I hate it had to end like this. You know, I didn't think it would take this long. The divorce proceedings, I mean. Not our marriage."

Eric nervously cleared his throat and adjusted his posture after seeing Noelle's pursed lips and furrowed brow.

"Look," he continued, trying to quickly remedy the situation. "I appreciate the generosity, but are you sure you don't want anything else besides the stuff you came in with? After all, you are legally entitled to any monetary assets gained during our marriage."

His tone was so flat and matter-of-fact, and that only aggravated Noelle more. It was like nails on a chalkboard.

"I'm positive, Eric," she said pointedly, straightening her already rigid posture. "Everything I've ever wanted, you gave to me willingly, and I'm grateful for that. However, there were some things I didn't ask for, like betrayal, heartache and misery. Those, along with the money, you can keep. As far as I'm concerned, you can use your money to buy an air conditioner for your new condo in Hell. Have a nice fucking day, Eric."

Noelle marched out of the courtroom with her head held high, and not once did she look back. She continued outside to the rented gray Toyota Camry in the courthouse parking lot and got inside, still prideful. But, the moment she pulled her left leg inside and closed the door, Noelle openly sobbed into her hands with her forehead pressed against the steering wheel. She cried because she was hurt...because she was ashamed...because she had failed. Noelle was like so many women who dreamed of the day their Prince Charming would come and whisk them away to live happily ever after. It would be such perfect bliss with love beyond measure.

Unfortunately, Noelle's fairytale soon turned into a nightmare that was far too much to bear physically, mentally and emotionally. She had lost weight, hair and for a frightful moment, her sanity. The amount of love and energy she had poured into her marriage in those two short years was more than she could spare, but she gave it without pause or complaint.

Now, as America sets off to spend the weekend celebrating its in-dependence, Noelle fears for hers. She would have to find a way to live without Eric, no matter how impossible it felt. She raised her head, wiping the mascara-tinted tears from her face, and accepted the fact that 'Noelle Pastor' was no more. She was Noelle Morgan once again, and she does not cry over a failed relationship. She moves on with her head held high.

Noelle pulled out of her parking space, heading to her suite at the Omni Hotel, courtesy of her lawyer. Tonight, she would order room service and watch the neighborhood fireworks from the balcony. In the morning, she would catch her flight to Houston, Texas and begin her life as a new divorcee. Noelle would give herself everything Eric promised but failed to provide. Yes, indeed! Today was Noelle's Independence Day.

One

Five Years Later...

The beautiful sunshine, serene sounds of birds singing and the light breeze of a gorgeous late-summer day all inspired the slight bounce in Noelle's step and the spontaneous whistling of Jill Scott's "Golden." As she strolled down the street towards work, she smiled cheerfully because something told her today was going to be a very good day. It had been five years since Noelle's divorce was finalized and she had moved back home to Houston. With each passing day since moving back, she made it her mission to regain her joy and vowed never to relinquish it again. Especially not to any man with nothing to add to her life.

Initially, she had to endure the sympathetic, yet smug, stares of other women in her hometown. Noelle Morgan held a long-standing reputation as one of the luckiest women in Houston when she started dating Eric Pastor her junior year at Texas Southern University. However, once word spread that she was leaving him, her pristine reputation became tainted. She was deemed silly, immature and a fool for walking out on such a "good man."

Once the real truth seeped out, some people's perception of her changed, but others still thought the act of infidelity was a forgivable offense when married to someone like Eric Pastor. Noelle couldn't understand that reasoning, and eventually she stopped caring about their opinions and questioning stares.

Since her divorce and move back home, Noelle bounced back better than anyone could've imagined. Three years ago, she opened her very own beauty salon in the Town Center shopping district of South Houston, aptly named *Noelle's*. She had also purchased a cozy three-bedroom house in a quaint part of the Pearland neighborhood that completed her "Living the dream" image.

As she reached the proverbial gateway to one of her lifelong dreams, Noelle gracefully pulled the salon's front door open and glided across the threshold with a wide smile still adorning her face.

"Good morning, ladies!" she sang the greeting to the staff and collective of customers as she entered the salon.

"Heeeyyy!" they replied in choppy unison.

"Mornin', Boss Lady," the receptionist said with a smile that matched Noelle's.

Debra Thomas was Noelle's right hand woman – had been since the shop first opened. She often wore many hats within the salon, stepping in to help with anything the staff and Noelle needed from her. Debra was a beautiful chocolate woman with perfect pixie facial features, full curly hair and small round-frame glasses perched neatly on her nose. She always had a warm smile and a kind word ready for anyone who needed it; but she also kept a healthy arsenal of pettiness on hand, just in case they needed that, too. It was the perfect balance that made Debra and Noelle the best of friends.

"Hey, Deb. Always a pleasure to see you doing some work," Noelle teased, playfully sticking out her tongue.

"Ha, ha!" Debra mocked, rolling her eyes and adjusting her

glasses. "What are you so chipper about this morning? Oooh! Was it a hot dinner date that turned into an even *hotter* breakfast date?"

Debra's question was accompanied by a devilish grin as she gleefully followed Noelle into her office, fully ignoring the way her boss had rolled her eyes. Noelle's office was a spacious room at the back of the salon with a large mahogany armoire on the left wall. Her desk matched it and was accented by a maroon, high-back tufted leather chair with gold buttons going down the middle of the chairback. The office had hardwood floors with one large floor-to-ceiling window that looked out into the shopping center's courtyard.

There were cream and gold sheer curtains hanging on the window, giving the office an elegant feel. A long couch matching the desk chair sat along the far right wall. Above the couch were three shelves that held framed photos of Noelle, her family and several with her co-workers at the annual Halloween and Christmas parties, but her favorite photo sat on her desk. It was a picture of her with the staff during the shop's grand opening.

As Noelle hung up her burgundy waist-length, leather jacket and chocolate-brown Coach handbag, she rolled her eyes again at Debra's earlier question.

"Whatever, Debra. Now let's get down to business," Noelle said dismissively as she perched herself on the corner of her desk, letting her left leg swing slightly back and forth. "What's on the agenda for today?"

Debra sat on the couch with her tablet in hand, as she did every morning to go over Noelle's daily itinerary.

"Well, you have an 11AM wash and roller set with Mrs. Burgs. Then at 1PM, Sonia Taylor is coming to get a weave overlay. She'll be supplying her own hair," Debra added with a snort and Noelle echoed the sentiment.

Noelle also had three sew-ins, two crotchets and a haircut appointment all scheduled for the day. On Tuesdays, she typically stayed open until 9PM instead of closing at the usual 7PM to allow for last minute walk-ins or clients who may be running a little late. By then, it was usually just Noelle and one other stylist – most often it was Debra who opted to stick around.

"Well, it sounds like we have a busy day ahead of us. So let's get to it!" Noelle gave a quick clap, breaking up their huddle.

She grabbed her navy blue wraparound smock with the salon's name in gold glitter lettering on the back and her name in cursive over the left breast pocket. Noelle walked out of her office, followed by Debra, and went to her station at the front of the shop, just as her 11AM client arrived.

"Good morning, Mrs. Burgs," Noelle greeted, spinning the chair around so the older woman could take a seat. "Right on time, as always. Come on so we can make you even more beautiful than you already are."

Mrs. Burgs bashfully smiled and waved her hand as she came over to the chair. The day ran smoothly from that point on. Each of the stylists stayed busy with their numerous appointments, but there was no over-crowding in the waiting area. Around 3PM, the customer traffic fluctuated from busy to mild then back to busy. Noelle was leading her next customer to the sink at the back of the shop to start washing her hair when she suddenly heard the front door's windchimes, signaling someone else's arrival.

Appreciative hoots and whistles could be heard coming from the customers and staff, but she didn't pay it much attention. They'd cut up like that when the mailman came in; so this was nothing new. As Noelle adjusted the water's temperature and fanned the customers hair under the warm stream, she heard her name come from an unfamiliar, but sensuously heavy baritone that unexpectedly sent chills up her spine, made her skin flush warm and piqued her interest.

Two

Two of South Houston's finest firemen had entered *Noelle's*, instantly receiving appreciative glances, catcalls and the occasional kiss blown their way. Like the gentlemen they were, they smiled graciously and even winked flirtatiously at the ladies as they walked up to Debra's desk. One of them held a binder and the other a clipboard.

"Good afternoon, Gentlemen," Debra greeted them with a warm smile, her sweet southern drawl pouring over each word like warm honey. "Welcome to *Noelle's*. How can I help you? I assume you're not here to indulge in any of our spa services."

"No, Ma'am. We're not here to indulge, but thank you," said the one with the binder. "We're actually just stopping by for your annual fire safety inspection. This is our last stop for the day, but that's not necessarily a bad thing,"

He looked around at the many pretty faces that openly admired him and winked at one of the female patrons, who swooned and fanned herself. The one with the clipboard was the next to speak.

"I'll have to agree with my partner here. But, I promise the inspection won't take long. We just need to see a Ms. Noelle Morgan," he said, peering down at his clipboard for confirmation.

At the sound of her name, Noelle turned to see who was asking for her. The fireman with the binder was a butter pecan complexion. He had short, curly cropped hair, thick eyebrows, full blushed-pink lips and a well-groomed mustache and beard. However, the true source of her curiosity was the man holding the clipboard. He looked every inch of six feet and four inches tall. He had a low cut fade with luscious waves that rippled across his head.

His face was clean shaven and flawless. His eyes were an odd shade of brown, like Sherry or Cognac, Noelle couldn't tell from the distance between them. His voice was what caught her attention the most. It was a sonically beautiful combination of Maxwell and Barry White. Not too deep to sound forced or intimidating, but deep enough to spark sensations within her that hadn't been felt in a long time. Her throat went dry and she got an anxious feeling swirling in the pit of her stomach.

Hearing Debra now call her name made Noelle snap out of her daze. She told her client she would be back shortly and asked one of her staff members to rinse the lady's hair and seat her back at her station. She walked to the front of the salon near Debra's desk where the two men stood. All the while, her eyes were locked on those of the one who piqued her interest the most. He was tall, muscular and the definition of masculinity in every way.

He had strong, toned arms with bulging biceps that fit snugly beneath the short sleeves of his uniform shirt. The expanse of his chest pressed ever so intimately against the shirt fabric, making the buttons look like they were struggling to keep his shirt closed. The navy blue shirt was tucked into matching pressed pants that hugged his strong thighs. The pants fell subtly over the tops of black, leather shoes shined to perfection and neatly laced and tied. His gold name badge and fireman's pin glistened in the mixture of the shop's fluorescent lighting and the late afternoon sunlight shining through the open blinds.

In true Noelle fashion, she approached with a pleasant smile that added a soft glint in her eyes.

"Welcome to my shop, Gentlemen," she said, extending her hand to each of them, her accent sweet and thick like molasses. "It is always a pleasure having fresh faces in this place."

"Thank you for being so gracious and inviting, Ms. Morgan. We hope this isn't too much of an inconvenience for you," the object of her attraction remarked.

"No need to be so formal. Please, call me Noelle. And I can't complain about your visit being an inconvenience, when I'm not exactly sure why you're here," she replied with a soft giggle.

The firemen chuckled slightly before explaining the reason for their visit.

"We just have to make sure all of your extinguishers are in standard working condition and easily accessible," the fireman with the clipboard said. "Make sure your smoke detectors and sprinklers are working properly, all exits are easy to get to, and be sure that none of your electrical cords or sockets are potential fire hazards. I'd hate for my next visit to involve me putting out any fires that could possibly destroy this beautiful place full of beautiful women."

He flashed a perfect smile, displaying pearly white teeth beneath luscious, delectably kissable lips...*Noelle, what is wrong with you! He's just a man! Get it together*! she silently scolded herself.

"Well, aren't you the charming one? Mister...?" Noelle asked, raising her perfectly arched left brow.

"Jackson. First name, not last," he said, smiling politely and touching his chest with the palm of his left hand. "And this is Aundre. Since we're being informal."

Pleasantries and smiles were exchanged amongst the trio, then Noelle escorted them throughout the shop to conduct their inspection. As she passed her waiting client, now seated back at her station, she apologized for the wait and assured her it wouldn't be too much longer. Noelle asked Debra to bring the young lady a complimentary cappuccino from the break room while she waited.

The first task on Jackson and Aundre's list was to inspect the placement and operation of all fire extinguishers. One was found on the wall at the back of the shop right outside of Noelle's office. Another on the wall by the front door and the third was upstairs in the nail technicians' loft. The next step was to assess whether all of the water sprinklers and smoke detectors worked properly.

When Aundre climbed the ladder to check the apparatuses in the hallway ceiling right outside the storage closet, Jackson took the opportunity to strike up a conversation with the cocoa-colored beauty beside him.

"So far everything seems to be in compliance and up to code. Good job," he said, looking down at her and offering a smile.

Noelle smiled in return and took the risk of looking into Jackson's inviting eyes. BIG MISTAKE! They were like deep pools of wonder and lust that temptingly tugged at every one of her feminine senses. Up close, she could see that his eyes were in fact a dark hazel color that seemed to darken the longer he looked at her. She inwardly wondered, *Does he have any idea how fine he is?...Why is he looking at me like that?...He better stop before he starts something!*

In the deep recesses of her mind, she pictured Jackson's muscular arms wrapped around her tightly; his strong hands caressing her face. She hadn't really enjoyed the touch of a man since her divorce was finalized. True, she had been on multiple dates with multiple men, but nothing ever came of those encounters other than erased voicemails and ignored phone calls. Noelle had found that most men weren't gentlemen anymore. They had so many ulterior motives that had nothing to do with treating her right, let alone committing to her.

Just thinking back on all those bad experiences disgusted her. It was like after her whole ordeal with Eric and his infidelity, she seemed to be a target for every wrong type of man there was. She had run-ins with everyone from the jobless ex-con to the lying married man. It had been a long, dry, unromantic five years for Ms. Noelle Angelique Morgan, to say the least. Yet, at this very moment while looking at the face of Jackson Lucas Howard she actually saw the potential for something...she just wasn't sure what.

The silence behind him caught Aundre's attention. He stole a glance at Jackson and Noelle and what he saw almost made him laugh out loud. They were like two lovestruck teenagers in that awkward, shy stage. As long as they had been friends, he had never seen Jackson look at any woman that way. *I think it's safe to say my boy has been hit by Cupid,* Aundre mused. That thought did make him laugh, which caused Jackson and Noelle to snap out of their trance.

Noelle blushed noticeably, while Jackson nervously cleared his throat. He excused himself from her side and walked over to Aundre, pretending to go confirm that the sprinklers were working okay.

"What are you over here giggling at?" Jackson asked in a hushed tone.
"I'm *giggling* at you, Lover Boy," Aundre said with a smirk.
"Whatever, man" Jackson said dryly, as he squinted his eyes in annoyance.

Jackson and Aundre concluded their inspection and congratulated

Noelle on successfully passing with flying colors. She thanked them and said they were more than welcome to return anytime for a leisurely visit, hair appointment or if they were looking for a date. Everyone in the shop laughed at her last comment, then farewells were exchanged as the two uniformed Adonises faded away into the distance. All the women released a unified and somewhat orgasmic sigh, then erupted in a fit of giggles and conversations centered around Jackson and Aundre's looks and even their potential sexual prowess. Noelle shook her head with a smile and went back to her long-waiting client.

After finishing up her last appointment, Noelle stepped into her office. The clock above the sofa read 6:30PM – two and half more hours until quitting time. Thankfully, she was pretty much done styling for the day. S0, she spent the rest of the evening going over inventory, invoicing and bookkeeping.

As she sat at her desk pouring over the weekly paperwork, her mind kept wandering in one direction...Jackson's. What was it about him that made his being so intriguing? It's not like she was able to get very acquainted with him. The man didn't really say much while conducting his inspection. Noelle wondered if he was just the strong silent type. Or maybe he was shy?

"That would be so cute," she thought out loud.

"*What* would be so cute?" Debra asked from the office doorway, making Noelle jump.

"How long have you been standing there?" Noelle asked, her eyes darting back and forth.

"Stop trying to change the subject! *What* would be so cute?" Debra asked again.

Noelle waved off her question and went back to her paperwork. Debra closed the door and tiptoed over to Noelle's desk. She stared at the top of her boss's head and smiled at her feeble attempts to avoid the conversation. Debra leaned forward and whispered in Noelle's ear, "*Him was cute.*"

Noelle's head shot up and she looked at Debra for a short moment before they both burst into laughter.

"Yes, *him* was!" Noelle said with a giggle. "My lord! I haven't seen a man *that* fine roaming around Houston in a long time."

"Me either," Debra happily agreed as she plopped down in one of the chairs in front of Noelle's desk. "Don't get me wrong. My hubby is a hunk in his own right, but damn! They both were fine as hell! *Especially* that Jackson."

Noelle couldn't help but agree. There was just something about the way he looked at her, and the way his body called to her and hers to him. It felt so natural. *Surely, you shouldn't feel this way about someone you've just met,* she thought. And yet, that is exactly how she felt. Her skin tingled at the very thought of Jackson. God forbid he ever actually laid a hand on her – her body might just melt away in his hands.

Noelle considered disclosing her inner thoughts to Debra, but resisted because she didn't want to blow her one chance meeting of Jackson out of proportion. After all, she doubted very seriously if she'd ever see him again, since there were plenty of firemen who could come by for a routine fire safety inspection. Noelle shrugged off the disappointment she felt at that thought. Then she and Debra continued to chat about some of the clientele that had come in earlier, and what the remainder of the workday had in store.

Closing time came sooner rather than later, which made Noelle very happy because she was exhausted. As she shut off the interior lights and stepped outside, she breathed a sigh of relief to be locking the doors to *her* salon and to soon be unlocking the doors to *her* home.

Three

Thursday morning came in with an eerie aura around it. Noelle woke up at 8AM like she did most mornings – showered, ate breakfast, and applied her makeup one eyelid at a time. However, this particular morning was unlike the rest. The early Fall air that was typical of late September was absent and in its place were much colder temperatures and heavy rains that beat down on the roof overhead. Noelle knew this time of year brought on a multitude of changes, but today just felt...different.

She woke up with this nervous feeling in the pit of her stomach, stiffness in her joints and a weird sense of foreboding, or worse...déjà vu. It had been a long time since she last felt like this, and that last time didn't end so well for her.

When Noelle finally arrived at the salon, she was greeted by Debra and two other stylists who had come in for early appointments. It was only ten minutes until the salon officially opened for business, and Noelle still wasn't feeling much like herself. A fact that wasn't lost on Debra, because she instantly furrowed her brow suspiciously when Noelle sluggishly walked in and offered the driest "Hello" Debra had ever heard.

She followed Noelle into the office as usual. Noelle hung up her coat and purse in the armoire, and grabbed her work smock, putting it on just as listlessly as she had walked into the shop. She never once made eye contact with Debra as they went through the routine of reviewing her daily schedule. When Debra finished going over the itinerary, she decided to address the proverbial elephant in the room.

"So, how long are we gonna pretend like there isn't something wrong with you?" Debra asked, her voice laced with concern.

Noelle shook her head in dazed bewilderment and shrugged her shoulders.

"Deb, I wish I could tell you what's wrong, but for the life of me I don't know," she replied dejectedly. "I woke up this morning with a sick feeling that I just cannot shake. And to be honest with you, it has me terrified."

Noelle dropped her head into her hands. Seeing her friend this way made Debra's heart ache. She walked around the desk and gave her a comforting hug. Noelle breathed a faint sigh of relief, but she still had an inkling of something bad happening today.

◇ ◇ ◇ ◇ ◇ ◇

Thursdays were one of the shop's busier days, because most of the clients were coming in trying to beat the anticipated traffic of Friday and Saturday's business. Noelle barely had a break between clients. After she'd put one under the dryer, the next one was sitting in her chair. She couldn't even pass off one of her waiting clients to any of the other stylists because they were all just as busy. When the midday rush slowed down around 4PM, She decided to make a break for it.

"Hey, Deb," Noelle called out as she approached the front desk. "I'm running down to BeBe's for a caffeine boost. You want anything?"

BeBe's Bakery was a small baked goods and coffee shop about four doors down from Noelle's salon that she frequented when the urge hit her.

"Ooohh! Yes!" Deb exclaimed.

"Write it down, because I'm not about to pop a blood vessel trying to remember your order," Noelle teased.

"It's not even that complicated," Deb replied, rolling her eyes and grabbing a Post-it Note.

"Yeah, yeah. Write it down anyway. I'm going to grab my coat," Noelle said with a chuckle.

The rainy morning had given way to gray skies and a crisp breeze. The sound of car tires slapping and splashing along the road and Noelle's heels clicking against the concrete sidewalk, melodically filled the air as she strolled down the street. The door chimed and the sweet, buttery smell of cinnamon rolls greeted Noelle as she stepped inside of BeBe's Bakery.

The cherry oak tables and countertops held up numerous patrons and their delectable sweets and drinks. The glass casing at the front of the bakery held every kind of cake, donut, pastry and bite-sized treat you could think of. The aroma of fresh ground coffee and flavored syrups swirled around Noelle's head like a delicious cloud.

"Noelle! What brings you in here?!" the owner greeted her with a smile.

"Hey, BeBe!" she replied, smiling back. "A desperate need for caffeine and business up to my eyebrows is what brings me in today,"

Noelle placed hers and Debra's coffee orders and opted for a box of a dozen mixed pastries to take back to the other ladies working in the salon. *The sugar rush will be welcomed, I'm sure,* she thought to herself. The chatter of fellow coffee drinkers, periodic chiming of the bakery's front door and faint sounds of soft coffeehouse jazz playing overhead were Noelle's soundtrack while she waited for her order to come up.

She was in the middle of replying to a text message from a client who was running late, when her hands abruptly froze. Her breath became trapped in her lungs, unable to escape. What little air she was able to expel, came out in a tremble. She couldn't bring herself to look up from her phone. She couldn't face the reality of the voice she swore she had just heard ordering at the counter.

Noelle was so engulfed by shock and disbelief, that she didn't even hear the clerk calling her name at first, signaling her order was now ready. She quickly shook it off and gathered her senses, readying to walk towards the counter. The strong smell of masculine heat and Burberry cologne rushed its way to Noelle's nose as she brushed past another patron on her way to collect her drinks and pastries. *That* was when she *knew.*

"Nola?" a deep, raspy voice called out her childhood nickname. "I heard the name 'Noelle' at first, but didn't think it was *the one and only.*"

Noelle took a deep breath, squared her shoulders and silently counted to three before turning on her heels to face *The Voice.*

"Hello, Eric," she said dryly, her jaw clenched and lips pursed.

Noelle was greeted by the strikingly handsome face belonging to none other than her ex-husband. Pools of hazel set in perfectly rounded orbs that rested atop equally perfect cheekbones. Cheekbones that were evenly painted a caramel color and accented by an expertly trimmed beard and mustache that framed one of the most beautiful smiles good dental care had ever paid for. None other than Eric Pastor. *Jesus!!*

"How have you been, Nola? You look good," he continued with a smirk.

"I've been busy. As a matter of fact, I'm *still* busy. Gotta go," Noelle said, grabbing the drink tray and box of pastries off the counter.

She walked by Eric as if he weren't even there and headed straight towards the door.

"It was good seeing you, Nola," he called out behind her, offering another warm smile.

"Aww, Eric. I'd say the same, but I'm not as good of a liar as you are," she said with a straight face before backing out of the bakery's door and disappearing down the street.

Eric chuckled to himself as his eyes followed Noelle until she was out of view. It had been awhile five years, to be exact – and he had to admit that time had been good to her...more like *great*! He wondered if it was really just a coincidence of them bumping into each other, or if it was something deeper than that.

Houston was a huge city. So, what were the chances that out of all the people he could possibly see in a coffee shop on the southside of town, he sees Noelle Morgan? *What are the odds?* Eric thought to himself as he took a sip of his piping hot, vanilla bean flavored coffee, staring out of the bakery's front window as if he could still see her standing there.

◈ ◈ ◈ ◈ ◈

Noelle entered the salon in a huff, mumbling angrily to herself. She practically slammed the drink tray and box of pastries down on the ledge of Debra's desk. Locking eyes with those of her confused friend, Noelle expelled a heavy sigh, making her nostrils flare wildly.

"You are not gonna believe who I just saw," Noelle said through gritted teeth.

"Who?" Debra asked, grabbing her latte from the tray and eyeing an almond croissant through the top of the pastry box.

"Eric," Noelle answered, her jaw still clenched.

"Eric? Eric who?" Debra asked, never taking her eyes off that croissant.

Debra lifted the top of the box, letting the smell of freshly baked goods waft across and around her desk. Just as she reached her hand inside to grab the almond croissant she had been eyeing, she realized Noelle never answered her question. Debra looked up and raised her brow.

"Eric, as in your *ex-husband Eric*?!" Debra exclaimed after reading Noelle's expression.

"The one and goddamn only!" Noelle fumed before going back to her office to hang up her coat.

The quick tapping of Debra's shoes could be heard behind Noelle as they both headed toward the office. Debra asked what happened and Noelle gave her all the details of their dry, yet heated, exchange. She had no idea why Eric was back in Houston or what were the odds that they'd actually run into each other. She literally hadn't seen him since the day their divorce was finalized. Even when she moved out of their condo in New York, she made sure to do so when he was not there. While Noelle was still close to his mother after all these years, she always managed to avoid him and any conversations about him. So, why the hell did her luck have to run out today?! *Just...why?!*

Noelle went back to work, trying hard to shake off the annoyance of having unexpectedly bumped into her ex-husband at BeBe's Bakery during her afternoon coffee run. *No matter what, the show must go on,* she encouraged herself. The hustle and bustle of customer traffic was back in full effect with clients pouring in after their workday ended. Lively chatter, water spraying and the low humming of hair dryers played a hectic symphony around Noelle as she tried hard to focus on putting the finishing touches on a sew-in for her client. Her mind was still racing and reeling from seeing Eric and she felt unsettled...just like she did this morning when she first woke up.

Was God trying to warn me about today potentially being shitty? Noelle thought. *Because it's definitely well on its way down the crapper.*

Noelle was in the middle of giving her next client, Ms. Eloise, a relaxer when she heard the familiar toll of the butterfly windchimes over the salon's front door. When she looked up, she saw a young man dressed in a light green delivery uniform carrying a bouquet of the most beautiful oriental lilies and wax flowers Noelle had ever seen. They were a glorious arrangement of purple, white and yellow flower blooms, accented by healthy leafy green stems that added to its fullness. Noelle silently wondered who they were for. Her ponders were answered when Debra called her name and beckoned her to the front.

"This young man has a delivery for you, and he needs your signature for confirmation," Debra explained.

Noelle was very perplexed, as she had no idea who would be so thoughtful and send her flowers at work. *Maybe they're from one of my clients as a "Thank You,"* Noelle thought. *Maybe they're from Debra, trying to cheer me up from earlier. Or maybe they were delivered to me by mistake.*

She tossed around every possibility she could think of, but something deep down said they were all wrong. There was something more...something reflected in every petal of every flower in that bouquet. She asked the delivery man if he knew who sent them, and he told her they were sent anonymously, but a card was attached that may offer a hint as to who the sender might be. Noelle signed his clipboard and thanked him. She studied the bouquet, admiring every bloom and smelling each flower as if committing their individual scents to memory.

Noelle picked up the vase and started carrying it to her office. As she went by, she heard a chorus of people clearing their throats to get her attention. She looked around the salon and all eyes were fixed on her.

"Y'all are so nosey!" she laughed.

"Well, who are they from?" one of the stylists asked.

"I have no idea, but there is a card that may give me a little hint," she answered.

Noelle pulled out the small white card with gold embossed lettering on the front that read "To You." She unfolded it and read aloud,

"As hard as I tried, I could not find the words to describe how beautiful you are to me.
These flowers are meant to be a mirror for you to see yourself through my eyes."

All of the women smiled and sighed blissfully at the romantic gesture.

"There's no signature or anything?" Debra asked from her desk at the front.

Noelle looked over the card once more, but saw no signs of who had just made her day. Then Ms. Eloise chimed in.

"That means you got a secret admirer, Baby. Some man has got a little crush on you," she said with a smile.

That is so sweet. I've never had a secret admirer before, but who could it possibly be? Noelle mused.

Four

⁓

Noelle woke up on cloud nine. Today, she felt more refreshed and well-rested than she'd had in weeks. Perhaps it was because the holiday season was fast approaching. Or maybe it was her joyful anticipation of being around her family this weekend to celebrate her older brother Richie's birthday. Partially, the latter may have been the case, but as Noelle skipped down the stairs from her bedroom to the kitchen she realized what really had her so giddy. In the center of the kitchen table sat a large bouquet of purple and white calla lilies that smelled divine. They had been this week's gift from her secret admirer with a card that simply said,

> *Brightening your day is the highlight of my week. Enjoy, Beautiful Lady.*

Every Thursday for the last three weeks, Noelle had received a delivery from *Gertrude's Garden Floral Shoppe* like clockwork. She smiled while re-reading all the cards on the refrigerator that were held up by fun ladybug magnets. She enjoyed reading her secret admirer's words, and desperately wished she knew their identity. A few people had crossed her mind after receiving the first bouquet, but now that she'd received a third delivery, it became harder to determine who her mystery suitor might be.

The cards never revealed a signature or any hints of identity, but

Noelle had to admit that she actually liked the not knowing. Nothing about her gifts seemed odd or threatening or even boded suspicion of a possible stalker. No, she honestly believed that someone somewhere had a secret crush on her and she found the prospect of that simply adorable.

Noelle returned to her bedroom to start getting dressed for work. She opted for a form-fitting, burgundy sweater dress that hung down to her knees with a shallow rounded neckline. She accented the dress with a gold chain waist belt that hung loosely around her slender midsection. Gold hoop earrings, gold bangles and brown knee-high leather boots with a slight three inch heel completed her ensemble.

Noelle assessed her wardrobe choice in the mirror and found it satisfactory. She grabbed her coat, purse, keys and travel coffee mug and headed out the door for work. She wanted to get to the shop early to finish up some last minute paperwork because she planned to leave a little early to go help her mom grocery shop for Richie's birthday dinner on Sunday.

◇◇◇◇◇◇

Noelle was sitting at the reception desk scheduling a customer for their return appointment, when she heard the front door open. She offered a courteous "Hello!" to the patron, but never actually looked up. Then she heard a sweet sing-song voice go, "Sissy!" and it touched her heart and brought a huge smile to her face. She let out a loud shriek and rushed into the arms of her baby sister, Shandra.

Shandra Morgan was the youngest of the Morgan children. At the tender age of twenty-two, she was currently attending the University of Texas-Dallas, pursuing a degree in Psychology. Shandra was such an animated personality. She was very outspoken and opinionated, perhaps even too much so and at the wrong times. She was also very protective of those she cared about – particularly Noelle.

In fact, Shandra was one of the first to come to Noelle's rescue when her marriage to Eric fell apart. It never sat well with Shandra that he wanted to whisk her sister hundreds of miles away from everyone and everything familiar for the sole purpose of advancing his own career and lifestyle. So, needless to say when Noelle called home confessing her marriage was over, Shandra was on the first thing smoking to her sister's rescue, along with their mother, Annabelle.

Since then, Shandra has harbored an intense hatred for her ex-brother-in-law and never bothered trying to hide it, but that whole experience really brought her and Noelle closer. Shandra even spent the summers working for Noelle when she was home from school. So, it was only right that she stopped by the salon once she got to town this time.

The two sisters finally released each other from their joyful embrace. Noelle held Shandra at arms length and gave her a good once-over.

"Shandy, you look great!" Noelle complimented, using her childhood nickname.
"Thank you, Girl!" Shandra replied with a smile. "You look fantabu-lous, as always!"

Noelle was so glad to see her sister again, it was such a wonderful surprise. She told Shandra to give her a minute to finish scheduling her customer and then they would catch up. While she waited, Shandra went around the salon greeting all the stylists she had grown close to over the last few summers. Once Noelle was done, she escorted her sister to her office so they could chat.

Shandra removed her coat, adjusted her green, fitted ribbed sweater and purple infinity scarf before taking a seat on the leather couch. She was slightly curvier than Noelle with wider hips, thicker thighs and bigger calves – all traits she could thank their mother for. Noelle had a more narrow waistline than her sister, but Shandra adored her "cushy middle," as she called it. She had auburn spiral curls that draped around her shoulders and framed her cocoa complexion that matched her sister's. Had it not been for the age difference, people would swear they were twins.

"So, tell me Miss College Girl, what's got you breezing into town?" Noelle asked.

"I couldn't miss Richie's birthday celebration," Shandra started. "You know he would never forgive me, and if I missed out on mama's cooking, I'd never forgive myself."

Noelle laughed at her sister's statement. This Sunday was their older brother, Richie's, thirty-second birthday, and their mother was planning a family dinner celebration. Noelle asked if she was only in town for the weekend, and Shandra said she was staying until Tuesday. The two sisters played catch-up for a little while longer until Noelle's next appointment came in, and Shandra opted to go upstairs to the nail tech suite and treat herself to a mani-pedi.

◇ ◇ ◇ ◇ ◇

Noelle was putting flexi rods in her client's hair when the salon door chimed and the appreciative catcalls and whistles from the customers and staff caught her attention. She turned towards the door and looked into the face of the fine specimen that had infiltrated her memory bank and wreaked havoc on her hormones for weeks...Jackson Howard, the fireman who had come in to perform her safety inspection about a month ago.

His partner, Aundre, was also with him, and the double dose of male sexuality and attractiveness was more than Noelle could handle at once, especially where Jackson was concerned. She let out a nervous giggle as she finished placing the last flexi rod and sprayed a hefty amount of holding spray onto the woman's hair before sitting her under the dryer. Noelle then walked up to Jackson and Aundre to greet them.

Jackson watched every step she took, he simply could not help himself. The way her feet danced so elegantly across the tiled floor intrigued him beyond comprehension. He had never really paid much attention to the way a woman walked before, but the way Noelle so gracefully put one foot in front of the other as she went just amazed him. Then the way her leather boots hugged her cocoa, smooth as silk calves; and the tantalizing way her thighs slightly peeked from beneath the hem of her dress with every stride; and the sway of her hips. *Oooh, those hips!* Jackson thought.

They weren't too wide or too narrow, but just right to highlight her femininity and accent the luscious curvature of her waistline. A waistline that called out so sweetly to his hands, inviting them to caress and commit themselves to igniting the flames of passion that would surely consume him. The sound of Aundre clearing his throat brought Jackson back to reality. It was then that he realized Noelle had been speaking to him, but he hadn't heard a word she said.

"I'm sorry. I didn't hear you. What did you say?" Jackson asked, slightly embarrassed.

Noelle smiled sweetly at him, enjoying the way his deep voice stroked her entire feminine being, and the way his southern drawl tugged at her heart strings.

"I asked, what brings you two gentlemen in today? Aundre said he'd let you answer that one," Noelle said.

Jackson looked over at Aundre, who had the most devious smirk plastered on his face. Jackson shook his head because he knew his friend clearly had an ulterior motive here. He looked back at Noelle to answer her question, but almost lost his nerve at the sight of her beautiful smile and enchanting eyes. Just as he was gathering his bearings and about to respond to her question, he saw another young woman coming towards them with a bounce in her step.

"Sissy! What do you think of this color?" Shandra asked Noelle, holding out her left hand to show off her french vanilla-colored nail polish.

Noelle told her it was cute, but the compliment that grasped her attention the most came from Aundre.

"It looks great on you. Compliments your skin tone nicely. I like your highlights too," he added, referencing the honey-blonde streaks in her hair.

Shandra looked at him with a raised eyebrow as a smile slowly crept across her face.

"Thank you, Sir," she said to Aundre, then she turned to Noelle. "Your clientele is so nice around here."

Noelle laughed and told her who they really were, and then introduced everyone.

"Shandra, this is Jackson and Aundre. Gentlemen, this is my little sister, Shandra."

The three of them shook hands, but Shandra allowed her hand to linger a while longer in the palm of Aundre's. The instant mutual attraction between them was very obvious to anyone with two eyes.

"So what brings two of Houston's finest into a hair salon?" Shandra asked, leaning into her sister.

"I asked the same question, but have yet to get an answer," Noelle replied, looking back and forth between Jackson and Aundre.

"Well, we just came back to bring you this," Jackson laughed as he handed her a manila envelope with her name on it.

She asked what it was and he explained that it was the results of her inspection they had performed and a certificate of completion. When asked why the department didn't just mail it out, Jackson stated matter-of-factly, "Because then we wouldn't have been able to come back and see all these lovely women."

He said it as a joke, but honestly Jackson just wanted an excuse to see Noelle's face again. He had agonized for weeks on how he could see her without it being awkward. So, when the opportunity presented itself, Jackson refused to miss his chance, and Aundre refused to miss out on seeing Jackson squirm in the presence of a beautiful woman. What Aundre hadn't planned on was doing a little squirming of his own. Shandra's beauty had not been lost on him at all.

Her gorgeous smile, curvaceous body, luscious hips and voluptuous thighs piqued his interest in the highest way. The moment she came bouncing so cheerfully down the stairs, something came alive in Aundre, and as intense as a lightning strike, it hit him...he wanted her like any red-blooded man could want a woman.

The quartet continued on in friendly conversation until the voice of the firechief came through Jackson's walkie-talkie paging all available firemen to report to a house fire nearby. Regrettably, Jackson and Aundre bid the ladies farewell before responding to the chief's call. Noelle and Shandra told them to be safe as they waved goodbye, then the two sisters shared a knowing look and giggled as the two men disappeared out of sight.

Five

〰

"That's odd," Noelle said to herself as she pulled into a parking spot across the street from her parents' house.

The driveway and curbside in front of their house was filled with cars of her relatives who had come by for her brother's birthday celebration dinner. On the opposite side of the street, Noelle even spotted a few other cars she recognized, but as she parked behind a shiny black Range Rover SUV with a New York license plate she became curious. It's not that abnormal to see out-of-state plates driving around the Houston area or even parked around her parents' neighborhood. Noelle just wondered which house they were visiting.

"That's a long ass drive," she chuckled to herself as she climbed out of her Lexus.

Noelle was so excited to see her family. With her being so busy at the salon lately, she'd missed out on the last few family gatherings. There was no way she was missing out this time. Plus Richie would never let her live it down if she did.

The sounds of joyous laughter and chatter washed over Noelle like a blissful wave when she walked through the front door of her parents' house. The mouth-watering smells of honey-baked ham, macaroni and cheese, lasagna, turnip greens and her mom's popular turtle brownies all beckoned her inside. As if that menu wasn't enticing enough, Richie personally requested Noelle make two of his favorite dishes by her – a key lime-strawberry pie and candied yams.

"You're so damned spoiled!" she had yelled at him when he called late Friday night with his last minute begging.

Noelle could hear the television playing in the den and knew that's where she'd for sure find her father. She slid the Chinese doors open and peeked her head inside.

"Hey, Daddy," she said cheerfully.
"Hey, Baby Girl," her father answered without taking his eyes off the television.

Richard Morgan had smooth, chocolate skin lightly decorated with freckles sprinkled across his cheekbones. His curly, salt and pepper hair glistened in the sunlight drifting through the window behind his favorite La-Z-Boy chair. He had a full beard that still had more black hairs than gray. His brown tortoise-shell glasses rested just so on the bridge of his nose and he had what some thought was a permanent scowl on his face, but Noelle knew he was really harmless.

Richard spoke with a heavy, slightly gruff voice that made people hesitant to challenge him or what he said. As a sixty-something year-old retiree, Richard J. Morgan made it a point not to do or deal with any-thing he didn't want to, and today was no different.

"Daddy, why are you hiding out in here when the party is out there?" Noelle asked, leaning down to kiss the top of her father's head.
"I ain't hidin'. I'm in here mindin' my bid'ness," Richard answered, still not looking away from the Houston Texans football game he was watching.
"But, you have guests in your house," she rebutted.

"No. Yo' brother got these people in my house. And they ain't no guests. Just ya cacklin' ass aunties," he replied.

"You better quit talking about my sisters like that, Richard James Morgan!" a stern voice called out from the doorway behind Noelle.

Annabelle Morgan, crossed the threshold into the den eyeing her husband disapprovingly before greeting her daughter with a hug and kiss on the cheek. Annabelle was a caramel complexion with light brown, curly hair, full and naturally arched eyebrows, brown eyes and smooth, blemish-free skin with a Marilyn Monroe-esque mole right above her top lip. She was a full-figured woman with plush hips and thighs that her daughters inherited and her husband couldn't get enough of.

After she and Noelle exchanged pleasantries, Annabelle swiped at her husband with the dish towel she was holding for the comment he made about her sisters.

"Ain't like I'm lyin'," Richard said to his wife over his shoulder. "They are her aunties and they're cacklin'. I don't see where I was wrong here."

"Whatever, crazy man," Annabelle said.

"But since you're in here, tell Noelle who all is out there."

"Richard," Annabelle snapped in an angry whisper.

For the first time, Richard turned his gaze from the television and locked eyes with his wife. With his eyebrows knitted in the middle and his voice firm, Richard simply uttered, "Annabelle," never breaking eye contact.

Noelle stood there, looking back and forth between her parents in confusion. She asked her dad what was going on and all he would say was, "Ya' mama's gonna tell you."

Richard continued to stare at Annabelle with silent and stern expectation, only breaking eye contact when he blinked slowly.

"Mama?" Noelle asked anxiously.

There was another long, silent pause that was eventually interrupted by Annabelle's heavy sigh before she spoke again.

"Marguerite is here," she finally confessed.

Noelle jerked her head back, blinking rapidly and swearing she had heard her mother incorrectly.

"What?!" Noelle exclaimed.
"Hmph," Richard grunted before turning his attention back to the television.
"Are you serious?! Wh-Why?!" she demanded.
"Noelle, please calm down," Annabelle pleaded, grabbing her daughter's arms.
"What is she doing here, Mama?!" Noelle asked angrily.

Annabelle explained that her niece, Marguerite, had recently moved back to Houston, and when she heard about Richie's birthday dinner, she jumped at the chance to be around her family again. Marguerite was the daughter of Noelle's favorite aunt, Gladys, who was Annabelle's younger sister. Gladys had mentioned the family getting together, and thought it would be a great opportunity for Marguerite to get to see everybody again...and Noelle couldn't disagree more.

"You have got to be joking," Noelle said in disgust.
"Noelle, it's your brother's birthday and the whole family is here. I get you're upset, but I'm asking you to play nice today. If not for me, do it for Richie," Annabelle pleaded.

Noelle scoffed at her mother's request. Searching her eyes to see if she was being serious, Noelle was crushed when she realized this was a legitimate ask. She was expected to set aside her feelings for the greater good of everyone else's comfort and to keep the peace.

"No," Noelle said in a breathy whisper, angry tears brimming in her eyes.

She pushed past her mother, heading out of the den towards the dining room where all the ruckus was coming from. Just as she rounded the corner, cutting through the living room, her brother came into view. Richie Morgan was the spitting image of his father, freckles and all, just thirty-years younger with less gray hair on his head. He was dressed in a black cable-knit sweater, black slacks, and black suede loafers with gold trim. He wore a gold herringbone chain around his neck and a matching Movado watch on his left wrist.

"Shit! Nola," Richie said under his breath at the sight of his sister.

He walked toward her, halting her march into the dining room. He clasped her hands that were still holding the dishes she'd brought.

"Oooh! Are these for me?" he said gleefully, trying to distract her.

For a split second it worked. Looking at her brother's smiling face and feeling his comforting touch, brought her blind rage down a bit.

"Hey, Richie. Happy birthday," Noelle said with a smile that didn't quite reach her eyes.
"Thank you, Sissy. And thank you for coming," Richie said.
"Of course I came, but now I don't know how good that is," she said, sounding annoyed.
"Yeah, I'm sorry about that. I had no idea they were coming," he apologized.

"They? Who's *they*?" Noelle asked, raising an eyebrow.

Noelle stormed into the dining room that was filled with her family milling about setting the table, putting the food out and finding their seats. The sounds of friendly conversation and glass dishes clinking together were abruptly interrupted by Noelle shouting, "What the fuck?!" as she entered the dining room. Everyone halted their movements and conversation and looked at her in shock.

"You have got to be fucking kidding me!" Noelle exclaimed.

"You watch your mouth in my house, young lady!" Annabelle said from behind her daughter as she made her way into the dining room.

Noelle cut her eyes at her mother as she walked by. She was seething with anger and tempted by violence. Everyone around the table looked back and forth between Noelle and the source of her displeasure like a volatile tennis match and anxiously waiting for it all to hit the fan.

"What is going on here?" Noelle pressed.

"Well, hello to you too, Cousin," Marguerite said with a sly smile.

"What the f..." Shandra said as she rounded the corner into the room joining everyone else.

Marguerite Douglas had a very fair complexion with light gray eyes and long, dark hair. She wore Bordeaux red lipstick and long mink eyelashes. She had dimples in both cheeks and not a single blemish in sight. Marguerite had always been a slender beauty with dainty, feminine features that she shamelessly used to her advantage in any given situation with the opposite sex. A fact Noelle remembered all too well.

"Shandra," Marguerite offered the singular greeting without a smile.

"I'm going to ask you again, what the hell is going on here?" Noelle repeated, her skin feeling hot with anger.

"Well, it's Richie's birthday. When Mama told me about the party, we just had to come," Marguerite replied, plastering that same condescending smirk back on her face.

"*We just had to come*? Who is *we*?" Noelle asked, narrowing her eyes.

Just then the kitchen door swung open.

"Hey, Nola." Eric Pastor, Noelle's ex-husband, emerged from the kitchen carrying a pan holding the ham her mom had cooked.

Seeing him here, helping set the table and socializing with her family made so many long-forgotten memories come rushing back like an unexpected tidal wave. He was absolutely the last person Noelle ever thought she'd see in her parents' house again.

"*Eric*?! Wh-What are you..." Noelle was in such disbelief that the question faded from her lips like a wisp of smoke as her finger stood suspended in air pointing at him.

"What in the entire fuck are you doing here, negro?!" Shandra shouted across the table as Richie grabbed her arm before she could lunge at Eric.

There was a bit of an awkward silence that followed Noelle and Shandra's questions. Either no one knew what to say or they just didn't want to say anything that might make things worse. Everyone except Marguerite, who thrived on drama and foolishness as a source of entertainment.

"Well, I guess we oughta let everyone in on the secret since we're officially back living here," Marguerite said, throwing her hands up in the air.

"Why do you keep saying *we*?" Noelle asked, angrily tilting her head to the side.

Marguerite looked back at Eric, a wider smile slowly creeping across her face. Eric's eyes widened and nervously darted back and forth between Marguerite and Noelle. Marguerite turned to face Noelle again and clasped her fingers together, resting her chin atop her joined index fingers. Just then, the chandelier above the table flickered against the large diamond ring on her left hand. Several gasps could be heard throughout the room, but Noelle could barely even breathe at the moment.

"We're engaged, Nola," Eric finally offered matter-of-factly, but barely making eye contact.

"You're *WHAT*?!" Shandra and Richie exclaimed.

"Well, shit!" their grandmother, Ernestine, said, shaking her head.

"Oh, my!" Aunt Gladys, Marguerite's mother, said with her hands covering her mouth.

Noelle stood frozen in complete silence. Not blinking. Barely breathing. Hands shaking. Skin feeling flushed. Knees growing weak. One lone tear trailing down her left cheek. Eyes locked on Eric's, speaking volumes only they could hear.

Annabelle rushed to her daughter's side, but Noelle flinched and recoiled at the touch. She looked into her mother's eyes trying to communicate the pain that lay inside her own. Noelle slowly turned her attention back to her cousin and her ex-husband – the newly engaged couple. Just the thought of that made her nauseous.

"Well, isn't anybody gonna congratulate us?" Marguerite asked, looking around the table. "Sorry, to steal your shine today, Cousin. Wasn't meaning to let the cat out of the bag at your party, but it's out now."

"You are so foul," Richie said, shaking his head.

"No, you're a bitch!" Shandra shouted.

"I'll take that as a compliment coming from you, Sugar," Marguerite said with a smirk and wink.

"Noelle, please say something," Eric pleaded, drawing everyone's attention to Noelle.

Blinking slowly, fighting back the remaining tears that threatened to spill out, Noelle took one exasperated breath and said, "Fuck both of you," before backing out of the dining room. She could hear people calling her name as she left the house, slamming the front door.

Six

The rumble of thunder and raindrops tap dancing on the roof roused Noelle awake. While adjusting her weary eyes to the darkness of her bedroom, she realized she had spent yet another full day in bed. Every day for the last four days, Noelle would wake up in tears, then she'd get so exhausted she'd fall back asleep. A few hours would pass, only for her to wake up and the cycle would start all over again.

Ever since Marguerite and Eric dropped their bombshell on the family, Noelle had been an emotional wreck. She'd been so out of it, that she couldn't even bring herself to get out of bed for work. Noelle had rarely missed a day of "reporting for hair duty" since she opened the salon three years ago. She would always feel so guilty having to cancel or reschedule her clients, but this week she had no choice...or any strength left.

Each passing day was filled with constant reminders of the ever-present truth – her cousin was marrying her ex-husband. Just the thought of that made Noelle sick! It's like she was reliving the most hellish day of her life all over again. That one day she had worked so hard to put it out of her memory. Yet, once again those two have managed to trash her entire resolve in the blink of an eye.

January - Nearly Seven Years Ago...

Noelle sat in her cosmetology class, trying desperately to focus. But, something kept nagging at the back of her mind and she felt very nauseous, with these nervous knots forming in her stomach and mild heart palpitations. Her mother would always say that's her female intuition letting her know something needed her attention. The problem was Noelle had no idea what that "something" could be. Did it have to do with Mama or Daddy? No, she quickly dismissed the thought. Richie or Shandy? Nope, not them either. What could it be then? Suddenly, it smacked her right in the face...Eric! Something wasn't right with him. But what?

Noelle looked at the clock on the wall behind her instructor. She couldn't wait another forty-five minutes for class to be over. She quickly packed up her stuff and made her exit from class without being too much of a distraction. Luckily, as soon as Noelle rushed out of the building, her bus was approaching. A twenty minute bus ride and seven unanswered phone calls later, Noelle arrived at her home feeling even more frantic and worried. She knew there would be no peace until she laid eyes on him.

She opened the front door and was greeted by the sound of soft jazz music playing unusually loud from the stereo system in the living room. Noelle tried calling Eric's name over the music, but got no answer. She shut off the stereo and called out to him again, but still nothing. Noelle walked slowly towards the hallway where she thought she heard muffled voices. The closer she got to her bedroom door, the more audible the voices became. It was the coupled voices of a man and a woman...coupled voices that sounded very familiar...ones that should NOT be coming from her bedroom.

Noelle slowly pushed open her bedroom door, only to be

greeted by the strong aroma of whiskey, her favorite vanilla candles and sex. Clothes and shoes were scattered carelessly around the room, and the painful sight of HER husband in HER bed with another woman! And the worst part of it all was that neither of them flinched when Noelle opened the door. She blinked rapidly, hoping that what she was seeing was just some twisted illusion – a figment of her imagination, but it wasn't.

It was all so real...so tragically REAL. Eric was in their marital bed having sex with her cousin, Marguerite. Never once did he separate himself from her long enough to even acknowledge Noelle's presence, let alone plead his case. Never once did he display a look of remorse, regret or apology. Noelle could almost swear she saw a smirk when she caught Marguerite's reflection in the mirror. There was this unmistakable expression of sheer victory and satisfaction. She even winked at Noelle, who stood immobilized and speechless in the doorway. There was nothing to say.

Noelle tore her eyes away from the two adulterers and looked at the framed wedding photo on the dresser. She stared long and hard at that picture, before she let out a maniacal chuckle as she turned and left the room. She walked slowly down the hallway, sliding weakly along the wall, shaking her head in disbelief and self-reprimand for trusting THAT woman to live under the same roof with her husband. Noelle grabbed her purse off the couch and walked out of the front door and down the block to the bus stop.

She sat inside the bus shelter and finally allowed herself to succumb to her emotions. The sadness, pain and blind rage she felt in that moment frightened Noelle, but she had to let it happen. And in a tidal wave of tears and pain-filled screams,

Noelle let it happen right there in the cold and rain on a New York City bus stop.

The worst part of it all was that Eric never once made an attempt to apologize or try to save their marriage. When Noelle threatened him with a divorce, all he said was, "Do what you gotta do." Marguerite never admitted to any guilt she felt for her actions, and Noelle wasn't the least bit shocked by any of it. She was so glad her divorce was mostly amicable and straightforward. No ugly court battles necessary, but it took Noelle five long years to fully recover from that tragic moment in her life. And in one day all her hard work was turned to dust by the same two people who had destroyed her world once before.

The loud grumbling of Noelle's stomach broke through the darkened silence and her reminiscing. She realized another full day had gone by without her eating. She looked at the alarm clock on her nightstand and it read 11:30PM. Every restaurant she could tolerate right now was closed and she was really craving junk food more than anything else. *Time for a late night Kroger run*, Noelle thought as she stretched her body beneath the covers before slipping out of bed.

◇◇◇◇◇◇

Noelle aimlessly perused the cereal aisle of *Kroger*, not even sure what she was looking for. Since arriving at the 24-hour grocery store by her house, she had tossed everything from avocado spread to string cheese to graham crackers into her handheld basket. Just randomly pitching items in as she went from one aisle to the next. She shuffled up to the shelf and grabbed a box of cereal, looking it over like it was the most unfamiliar thing she had ever seen.

◇◇◇◇◇◇

Jackson grabbed a shopping cart from the front of the store and pushed it through the produce section of *Kroger*, trying to remember just what the hell he had come in there for?!

"I knew I should've made a list," he chastised himself, knowing full well he would never actually make a list.

Every time he'd say he would and every time he'd forget and just end up wandering the store cluelessly, as usual. Just then he remembered he needed some coffee creamer and pushed the cart along while peering down each aisle, searching for the item. Jackson took a quick glance down the cereal aisle and continued on, but stopped suddenly. He looked over his shoulder towards the aisle he had just passed, wondering if his mind was playing tricks on him.

Jackson backpedaled with his brow furrowed, and looked down the aisle again. Before his eyes could fully register what he saw, that familiar rhythmic thumping of his heart and flutters in his stomach told Jackson all he needed to know, and a joyous smile crept across his face as he walked towards the object of his attention.

Noelle was so enthralled with the box of cereal she was holding that she didn't even notice someone else in the aisle with her.

"*Honeycombs? Seriously?*" Jackson asked, breaking her concentration.

Immediately recognizing the voice and familiar musky scent of cologne and aftershave, Noelle's eyelids fluttered shut and she smiled for the first time in four days.

"Is that judgment I hear in your voice?" Noelle asked, looking at Jackson out of the corner of her eye.

"It absolutely is," Jackson replied, still smiling.

"I don't need your negativity, Sir."

"You're the one considering a box of *Honeycombs* cereal as a good choice at twelve o'clock at night. Negativity is already upon you, Ma'am."

Noelle exhaled a laugh as she turned to fully look at Jackson for the first time. Seeing his handsome face and warm smile was such a welcomed sight. He was dressed down this time in a black hoodie and sweatpants with a black Houston Astros fitted cap turned backwards. He wore a pair of black and white high top Nike sneakers, and Noelle noticed for the first time that he was slightly bowlegged. Unconsciously, she bit her bottom lip, thinking about how much sexier he had just become to her. Her eyes trailed further up and down his body, drinking in the full sight of him. *JESUS*! she thought to herself.

"Whatever, man!" Noelle finally responded with a soft chuckle, locking eyes with Jackson again. "Could be worse. I could be getting *Corn Flakes* or *Total*,"

Jackson clutched his chest and looked at her in pain, saying how grateful he was that her taste in cereal wasn't *that* bad. They finally got around to exchanging real greetings and finding out why they both were lurking through the grocery store so late at night. Jackson's shift at the firehouse had just ended at eleven o'clock, and since he would be off the next two days, he wanted to grab some things now instead of later.

"Wait, your firehouse is in this neighborhood?" Noelle asked.
"Yeah, not too far," Jackson said as he pushed his cart along.
"Where is it?" she pressed.
"On the corner of Walker and Polk," he said, throwing a loaf of honey wheat bread in the basket.

He started pushing the cart again, but realized Noelle was no longer walking beside him. He stopped and turned around to see her standing still, looking quite perplexed.

"What's wrong?" Jackson asked with concern in his voice.

"*That's* the station you work at?" Noelle asked in surprise.

"Yeah. Why?" he asked, narrowing eyes and tilting his head.

"That's down the street from my house," she revealed.

"Wait, *seriously*?"

"Yeah, my house is literally in the next block."

"You mean the woman of my dreams has been a block away from me this whole time?!"

"Well, I don't know about the woman of *your dreams*, but that's where *I* live, yeah."

"Ha, ha. Very funny."

Jackson walked Noelle to her car after they finished shopping, enjoying the light and playful banter between them. He didn't want any of it to end and knew if he didn't take this chance now, he'd probably never get another one.

"So...Noelle," he started.

"Yes, Jackson?" she replied, closing the trunk of her car after placing the grocery bags inside.

An intensely pregnant pause hung in the air between them as they looked into each other's eyes. Carrying on a full conversation without ever opening their mouths. Asking and answering one question after the other while never uttering a single word. Inviting one another inside their soul with the beckoning of every blink. Jackson reached out to brush a wisp of hair from Noelle's face, and she shuddered slightly at the touch. Jackson's lips formed a small smile of satisfaction.

"Would you like to go out with me tomorrow?" Jackson finally asked.

"Y-you want to go out...with *me*?" Noelle asked with sincere surprise.

"I've never wanted anything more," he said earnestly.

For a brief moment, Noelle hesitated. Her initial gut reaction was to politely decline...to take her sour mood and cookie dough ice cream back home and forget all about Jackson Lucas Howard, but she wouldn't. She couldn't. A small voice inside even assured her that she shouldn't have to. So she didn't.

"Yes, Jackson. I'd love to go out with you."

Seven

~

"Noelle!" a voice called out to her.

Noelle had been so lost in her flirty text exchange with Jackson that she hadn't heard her name being called from the doorway of her office. She snapped her head up and saw Tiffany, one of her stylists, standing there laughing at her.

"Huh?!" Noelle finally replied, her eyes wide with shock. "Sorry, Tiffany. How long have you been right there?"

"Thirty seconds at the most," Tiffany said.

"Oh, okay," Noelle exhaled.

"But don't ask how many times I've called your name, though."

Noelle gave a small grimace as the two of them started giggling. Tiffany asked who had captured her boss's attention so much and smiled with glee when she learned it was the sexy fireman from a few months ago.

"Well, I hate to interrupt, but you have a walk-in," Tiffany said, finally getting around to why she had come to the office.

"A walk-in? Oh, let one of the newbies take her so they can build up clientele," Noelle replied, checking her reflection in the mirror on the armoire door.

"She specifically asked for you," Tiffany replied.

"Really? She look familiar?" Noelle asked, lifting a single brow.

Tiffany shook her head and Noelle said she'd be right out. She sent another quick reply to Jackson before walking out of her office towards her station. Noelle switched her phone to vibrate and slid it into her back pocket. Just then she halted her steps when she saw who was sitting in her chair and using the handheld mirror to apply lipstick. A furious scowl came across Noelle's face as she marched towards her station.

"You must be out of your mind! What the hell are you doing here?!" Noelle asked angrily with her hands on her hips.

"My dear cousin, you must find a better way to greet people," Marguerite said as she wiped a smudge of lipstick from the corner of her lip with a dainty finger.

"Girl...fuck you!" Noelle exclaimed. "Now, *what* are you doing here?"

Marguerite finished assessing her reflection before swiveling around to face Noelle. She looked her cousin up and down, trying to see what everybody else saw in the "Golden Child" that is Noelle Morgan? Besides her wide hips and big butt, there wasn't much to look at, in Marguerite's opinion. Even back when Noelle and Eric were dating, Marguerite couldn't understand what he ever saw in her, and then when they got married she knew it wouldn't last long...not if she could help it, anyway. *And five years later, ain't life grand! I got exactly what I wanted,* she often praised herself.

Marguerite moved a small wisp of hair out of her face with one perfectly manicured fingernail and let out a heavy sigh.

"Well, as if it isn't obvious enough, I'm here to get my hair done," she said matter-of-factly. "Specifically, to do my hair trial for my wedding,"

Noelle's head snapped backward as if she had been smacked in the face. Her eyelids fluttered rapidly and she literally bit her tongue to curb herself from letting the curse words fly. After a series of many deep, calming breaths, she finally spoke.

"You *cannot* be serious," Noelle snapped through pursed lips. "What would make you think *I* would do *your* hair for *your* wedding to *my* ex-husband? Are you insane?!"

"Look, you really need to let that go," Marguerite said in annoyance as she turned the chair back around to face the mirror. "It's been long enough. I need my hair done and you need the money. So let's just get on with it,"

Noelle grabbed Marguerite's *Gucci Hobo* purse off the counter and shoved it into her chest as she jerked the chair around to face the center aisle of the salon.

"You can get up and leave on your own or I can drag you out," Noelle said forcefully while pointing towards the door. "Either way you're leaving my shop. Only choice you have is the how."

"Are you serious? I'm a paying customer and *this* is how you act?" Marguerite asked incredulously.

"At *Noelle's*, we reserve the right to refuse service to any and everyone, because we know that all money ain't good money and peace of mind is more valuable. Now get!"

Marguerite shook her head in disbelief and left the salon in a defeated huff. Noelle instructed the staff to remember her face because she was never allowed to enter *Noelle's* for anything ever again. Noelle was so angry she could feel her whole body violently shaking with rage. She rotated and cracked her neck, wrists and knuckles. Partly to release the tension there, but also just in case Marguerite decided to come back, there wouldn't be any more talking!

Noelle felt her phone vibrating in her pocket. Pulling it out, she saw two unread messages. One was from Shandra letting her know what time she'd be arriving by train. Today was the Friday before Shandra's school went on a week-long break for Thanksgiving. So she decided to come home today to extend her visit a little. Noelle had to pick her up from the station since Shandra would be staying with her half the time and the other half at their parents' house.

The second text was from Jackson: "*You…Me…Dinner tonight at 7PM. I'll pick you up. You know, 'cuz I'm such a gentleman and all,*" and it was punctuated by a kissy face emoji.

A huge smile spread across Noelle's face, as if the whole exchange with her cousin never happened. She instantly got excited just thinking about it. Noelle and Jackson hadn't had much opportunity for a solid date night in weeks. Their very first date was a simple lunch at what happened to be both their favorite bistro, and they'd had a movie date Halloween weekend because they wanted to see something spooky together. But after that, their schedules got so hectic that they ended up like two ships passing in the night.

To make up for it, they would try to briefly meet up for coffee or ice cream just for an opportunity to see each other. But, now they were going on a real date! *I get to dress up and be cute!* Noelle thought.

She did a quick happy dance and immediately started visualizing her wardrobe options in her closet at home.

◇◇◇◇◇◇

"Wait! You've been seeing this man for how long?! And why I ain't know?!" Shandra shrieked from the passenger seat as she rode home with her sister.

Noelle got her all caught up on the recent romantic developments between her and Jackson. Though things had been progressing slowly and carefully, she was so excited to see where they'd lead, because she was seriously enjoying her time with him. When they arrived at Noelle's house, Shandra ordered her sister to get in the shower and leave everything else to her.

"What?!" Noelle asked, both confused and concerned.

"I'm on hair, makeup and outfit duty, Ma'am. I have the chance to help my only sister get ready for a real date. Do not rob me of this moment! Now get!" Shandra replied, pointing towards the stairs, trying to maintain her stern expression.

Noelle stuck out her tongue and rolled her eyes as she ascended the stairs to follow Shandra's commands. An hour and a half later, Noelle was putting her jewelry on and spritzing herself with Marc Jacobs' *Daisy* perfume when she heard the doorbell ring. Shandra shouted up the stairs that she'd get the door while Noelle finished getting ready.

"Well, well, well," Shandra said as she opened the door and saw Jackson standing there holding a single, long-stemmed red rose.

"Hello to you too, Ms. Shandra," Jackson greeted her, smiling politely.

It still amazed him how much she and Noelle nearly had the same face, but he certainly knew which was his favorite. Shandra let him inside and said that Noelle would be down shortly.

"Jackson, can I be candid with you?" Shandra asked in a serious tone.

"Uh oh! Is this the 'what are your intentions with my sister?' conversation?" he asked playfully, placing his hand on his chest.

"Glad you know! Makes this easier for me," she replied, trying to hide her smile.

"Yes, Ma'am. I'm listening," he said, shoving his free hand in his pocket and fixing his eyes on hers.

"I'm not sure how much of her story my sister has shared with you, but just know she is precious to me, and I don't take kindly to others misusing and abusing her or her heart. So, if you mean her no good, leave her here. Now, I feel like I can trust her in your hands. Don't prove me wrong. Understand?"

Jackson stepped towards Shandra and extended his right hand. As their two hands connected in a firm handshake, he simply said, "Completely." He saw Noelle coming down the stairs out of the corner of his eye and lost his breath as his hand slid from her sister's grasp. Shandra saw where his gaze went and stepped out of the way so the two of them could get to each other. Watching the way Noelle's face lit up at the sight of him and how Jackson's eyes grew dark and hungry at the sight of her – all of it gave Shandra great hope that they were going to be good together.

As promised, Shandra put together a winning date ensemble. She had picked out a black form-fitting, long-sleeved, mock-neck sheath dress with a small slit cutout right across the décolletage. Shandra had pulled Noelle's hair up into a neat bun with a few ringlets falling around her face. Neutral makeup with a burgundy ombré lip, silver teardrop earrings, matching bejeweled bangles on each wrist and strappy black heels completed Noelle's date night ensemble.

Apparently great minds think alike, because Jackson was dressed in a simple black dress shirt with the top button undone to show off a silver cross necklace and a peek-a-boo of his smooth chest. He wore black slacks and midnight blue suede loafers. A shiny, Armani Xchange watch with a silver band and diamond bezel adorned his right wrist and a silver link bracelet on his left. Signs of a fresh haircut and neatly trimmed beard he had grown out for the colder season brought his whole look together. *He looks delicious!* Noelle thought.

"You look..." Jackson's words trailed off as he stepped closer and grabbed her hand, twirling her around to get a full view before kissing her softly on the cheek and handing her the rose.

Noelle thanked him for the flower and his unspoken compliment. She gave Shandra a kiss goodbye as she grabbed her cashmere poncho and clutch and followed Jackson out the front door.

Jackson held the door open for Noelle as she stepped inside the warmly lit Italian ristorante, *Arturo's*. The sounds of intimate chatter and clinking wine glasses mixed with the soft classical music playing overhead. The delectable aromas of pasta primavera, lasagna and finely prepared steak dinners wafted through the air, swarming around Noelle's head as she followed Jackson and the maitre'd to their table. The manager happened to be a friend of Jackson's and worked some magic to get them a private dining room overlooking the pier with a complimentary bottle of champagne.

Noelle shuddered at Jackson's fingers brushing against the thin fabric of her dress as he helped remove her poncho. She stole a glance at him as he pulled out her chair and draped the coverup over the back of it. His beard and mustache were neatly trimmed, leaving his neck clean shaven and so inviting. Noelle quietly wondered if he tasted as chocolatey as he looked and unconsciously licked her lips at the thought. She sat down, adjusted the napkin in her lap and appreciated the sight of Jackson's rear end as he walked to his seat across the table from her.

Their waitress came to go over the dinner and wine specials for the evening as she poured two glasses of iced water for them. When she walked away to give them a few moments to pour over the menu, Jackson took a sip of water before he spoke.

"You look amazing tonight, Ms. Morgan," Jackson said sweetly, finally stating his full compliment from earlier.

"Why, thank you, Mr. Howard," Noelle replied with a smile and glint in her eyes. "You clean up pretty nicely, yourself. Black is definitely your color."

"Looking at that dress on you, I'd beg to differ. Emphasis on *beg*," he said with wink.

Noelle gasped as her skin flushed warm at Jackson's suggestive words. She shook her head and smiled because he had temporarily left her at such a loss for words. Their flirty banter continued like a saucy tennis match across the dinner table as they hid coyly behind their menus. Eventually, they ordered their meals and paired them with a highly recommended red wine. A comfortable silence fell over the table as they indulged in their small feast.

Jackson reached over to refill Noelle's wine glass and then his own. She held the glass loosely in her hand, swirling around the red liquid before taking a sip. As it washed over her palette, it gave Noelle the boost of courage she needed to pose her question.

"So," she began. "Tell me something about you that I don't already know."

"What new thing would you like to know?" Jackson asked, peering at her over the rim of his wine glass.

"How many siblings do you have?" she asked with a shrug.

"Well, I'm my mom's only child, and don't really know my dad that well, but I've heard he has five other kids somewhere. So, five, I guess," he explained.

"Hmm, an only child raised by a single mom. Sounds like you were spoiled," she teased.

"Raised by a single mom *and* my granny. Spoiled as hell!" he confirmed with a chuckle.

"Fantastic! Sounds like I got my work cut out for me."

"I give as good as I demand."

Jackson tossed Noelle another wink across the table and it made her laugh out loud. They talked more about their childhoods – hers in Houston and his in Memphis, where he was originally from. She learned about his glory days of being an All-City football star at his hometown high school and an even bigger prodigy in college. When asked why he didn't pursue a professional career, Jackson explained that he did a brief stint in arena football, but decided he wanted something a little more stable, personally and financially.

"And what's more stable than a life of running into burning buildings?" Noelle said jokingly.

"Exactly! You get it," Jackson replied.

"Oddly enough, I do," she said.

"The fact that you understand how my mind works should probably scare you a little," he said with a smirk.

"Oh, I'm absolutely terrified, but also a little intrigued," she said, biting the corner of her lip.

The waitress arrived at their table with a complimentary dessert platter, courtesy of Jackson's friend, as well. It had a variety of bite-sized pastries, chocolate covered strawberries and cheesecake squares. Jackson popped the cork of their gifted champagne and paired it with the desserts. As the waitress cleared their plates from the table and gave them new sets of silverware, Noelle got a frisky idea.

She got up from her chair and walked around to Jackson's side of the table, motioning for him to scoot his chair back just a little. When he put enough space between himself and the table, Noelle slid between his legs and perched herself on his right thigh. She threw her left arm around his neck and arched her back slightly when she felt Jackson's arm wrap around her waist. Noelle picked up one of the forks, pierced the corner of a turtle cheesecake square and fed it to Jackson.

Noelle watched intently as his lips wrapped around the prongs of the fork and how his tongue swiped between and across his luscious lips. She toyed with the idea of following its path, but decided to let the dessert platter be the only sugar shared between them right now. Mostly because she knew that if they started, they'd never stop and would make an entire spectacle in these people's restaurant.

Jackson buried his nose in her neck, inhaling her heavenly scent between bites of dessert, while tracing circles on the small of her back with his middle finger. Noelle gently massaged the back of his neck as she hand-fed him a chocolate covered strawberry. Jackson picked up one and fed it to her next, kissing the corner of her mouth as the juice ran down her chin. She tilted her head to give him more access to her mouth, but he just tilted it back down and kissed his way along her jawline up to her temple. Though it wasn't what she was hoping for, Noelle welcomed the gesture just as happily.

The remainder of their date was spent with Noelle still perched in Jackson's lap – neither of them wanting that to change – as they polished off the rest of the dessert platter and bottle of champagne. Eventually, the waitress brought the check and the twosome took that as their cue to take their exploits elsewhere. As Jackson helped Noelle with her poncho, he took another opportunity to inhale her sweet scent. He quietly moaned to himself at the thought that she probably tastes just as good as she smells, if not better – a fantasy that immediately sent his blood coursing hot through his veins.

"I had a great time tonight, Jackson," Noelle said.

After dinner, they had gone to a lounge for some drinks and slow, close-contact dancing for a few hours. Now they were coming up Noelle's block after going for a walk because neither wanted the night to be over yet.

"I know we kept missing each other and not getting a lot of time together. I was sick of it!" Jackson said with a chuckle.

"I'm glad you said it, because so was I!" she replied with a giggle.

Noelle was truly enjoying not only Jackson's company, but also the feel of his strong hand as it held hers while they walked. The way his body heat just radiated off him and warmed her from the outside in. Those moments of comfortable silence that filled the air between them. It was all so blissfully satisfying.

They reached the front steps of Noelle's house, and both exhaled their sighs of disappointment at their date officially being over. Jackson helped Noelle up the steps to her front door and appreciated the way she let her hand linger in his for a bit. They made plans to see each other again within the next few days before they got bombarded by relatives during the holiday. Jackson kissed the palm of Noelle's hand he had been holding and then kissed her knuckles softly before telling her to go inside before her sister hunted him down for keeping her out too late.

Noelle turned to grab the knob of the screen door, but paused for a second. She had this question plaguing her mind for weeks and couldn't ignore it anymore. She spun on her heels to look at Jackson, who was still standing on the steps leaning against the banister.

"What's wrong?" he asked with concern in his voice.

"Jackson...why haven't you kissed me yet?" she probed.

It had been over a month of them hanging out, going on dates and getting to know each other. They got along great and the flirting was always off the chain. But, he still hadn't kissed her. Forehead, hands, cheeks, even the top of her head, yes, but never her lips...and she'd officially had it!

"I mean, do you even like me?" Noelle asked with a twinge of sadness in her eyes and voice.

"I'm crazy about you," he said pointedly.

"So then...why?"

"You really wanna know?"

"Yes, I'm dying to know!"

"Because you haven't given me permission to."

"What?"

"Noelle, I'm ridiculously attracted to you and want nothing more than to kiss you all the time. But, I'm not going to invite myself to your body in that way, as tempting as it is. I respect you too much for that. So, I'll wait."

Noelle looked at Jackson with fresh eyes at that moment. Before, he was this handsome, funny, gentle-spirited man who made her feel more like a woman than she'd ever had in all her twenty-something years. But, tonight was different. To learn that he was delaying and denying himself something as simple and pure as a kiss out of genuine respect for her and her boundaries, even without her asking, just made him that much more beautiful in her eyes.

It warmed her heart and touched her soul deeply. Noelle stepped towards Jackson as he stood one step below her. She looked deep into his dark hazel eyes and could see the question and request that lay within them. But, Noelle decided to ask one of her own instead. She brought her hand up, cupping the right side of his face and stroking it with the pad of her thumb. She leaned in closely so their noses and breaths touched intimately.

Noelle's eyes dropped down to Jackson's lips and she saw his tongue dart out and lick them in nervous anticipation.

"Jackson..." she beckoned softly.
"Yes, Love?" he replied, his voice deep and heavy.
"May *I* kiss *you*?"
"Please."

Their lips touched softly at first, and then all the pent up passion finally boiled over. The lusciousness of their lips became married together as their tongues danced sensually. Jackson gripped her waist tightly with his strong hands and moaned deeply against her mouth. Noelle caressed his face and head tenderly. Their breathing fell into a rhythm and their bodies followed. Jackson brought his hands up to cup her face. She gripped his forearms as their kissing slowed.

Pressing their foreheads together, they rode out the high that came from their first kiss. Definitely worth the wait.

Eight

"Noelle! Hurry up! Richie keeps texting me asking where we are!" Shandra yelled upstairs at her sister.

They were readying to head to their grandmother's house for Thanksgiving dinner. The Morgans and Douglases often rotated the big holidays like Thanksgiving and Christmas between their respective families. This year, Annabelle's side of the family – The Douglases – got Thanksgiving. She and her sisters met up early that morning at their mother's house to start cooking or heating up the pre-prepped dishes they had made at home. The menfolk often congregated out in the garage to yell at the football game on television and deep fry the turkey – a staple in the Douglas-Morgan Family Thanksgiving tradition.

Shandra and Noelle were on their way over at the request, or rather the demand, of their brother, and for once, Shandra was actually ready first and rushing Noelle to hurry up. Richie hated being the only "kid" at the house because his parents, aunts, uncles and Granny would run him ragged with all their "Hand me," "Bring me," "Pass me," and "Carry this" requests.

"Tell Richie to suck it up, and don't rush me!" Noelle said as she descended the stairs.

She was dressed in a charcoal gray, fitted cowl neck sweater, black faux leather knee length skirt with black mid-calf Coach riding boots and a black waist belt with silver buckle. Her hair was straightened under a black faux leather headband. She grabbed her burgundy vinyl jacket from the closet next to the stairs, and as she slid her arm through one sleeve, Noelle noticed Shandra's outfit.

"Uh, Ma'am!" Noelle shouted
"What?" Shandra asked, trying to feign innocence.
"Is that *my* dress?" Noelle asked, lifting one brow.
"Is it?" Shandra replied in a high pitched voice, looking down at the dress hugging her frame.

It was a chocolate brown, ribbed sweater dress with slits on both sides that stopped right at midthigh. It had a deep v-neckline with gold buttons across the shoulders. Shandra complemented the dress with tan knee high boots and gold jewelry. She loved this dress. It was probably one of her favorites that Noelle owned.

"Keep it, heffa," Noelle said with a smirk, shaking her head.

Shandra smiled so big and wide that Noelle couldn't help but laugh as they headed out the door.

◇◇◇◇◇

"Finally!" Richie Morgan shouted at his sisters when they entered their grandmother's house.

He was carrying a 42-inch flat screen television down the stairs, visibly frustrated.

"Where you going with that TV, Uncle Pete?" Shandra asked jokingly, referring to the reclusive uncle from the movie *Soul Food*.
"Ha, ha. *Y'all* uncles and Daddy are getting on my nerves!" he huffed,

rolling his eyes. "They wanna watch the game on a bigger TV than that 24-inch Granny has outside. So, guess who's lucky enough to go fetch them one?"

Richie rolled his eyes again and groaned in frustration talking about his male elders, then greeted each of his sisters with a quick kiss on the cheek. He pointed them towards the kitchen when they asked about their mom. Shandra stopped to hang up their coats in the hall closet while Noelle followed the rowdy sounds and delicious smells coming from her grandmother's kitchen.

The second Noelle pushed the swinging door open she was met with warm smiles and hearty greetings. She hugged and kissed her aunts, Gladys and Carolyn, who stood on opposite sides of the kitchen island prepping multiple dishes for the oven. Her mother, Annabelle, was at the stove stirring a large stockpot of greens and ham hocks that smelled divine. Annabelle's face lit up at the sight of her oldest daughter, who she hugged tightly as always.

"Hey, Baby Girl. You look good!" Annabelle said, giving her an appreciative once over.
"Well, I look just like you. So, I can't help it," Noelle said with a wink.

Noelle asked what she could help with and her mom told her to start the sweet potatoes. So, she grabbed the bag of potatoes, a knife and cutting board and set to work next to her mother. These moments were what Noelle looked forward to the most at family gatherings. Just being surrounded by generations of women in her family made her heart smile.

Shandra finally made her way into the kitchen after having stopped in the garage to say "Hey" to the menfolk. They barely turned away from the television, so she doubted they even heard her. She started snacking on an apple turnover Aunt Carolyn had just taken out of the oven and instantly got fussed at for not helping with the actual meal.

"Cook. College student. See how the words are different?" Shandra replied sarcastically. "I know my ministry, thank you very much,"

Annabelle was starting on the cornbread when she took the opportunity to get in her other daughter's business.

"So, Nola," she started. "You got a man now, huh?"
"What?! Who told you that?" Noelle asked, her voice full of shock.
"Um, that would be me," Shandra offered from across the room with a nervous smile on her face.
"Now why would you tell her that?!" Noelle asked, annoyed.
"Because it's true," Shandra said with a shrug.
"Don't try to change the subject, lil girl!" Annabelle chimed in. "Now, who is this young man?"

Noelle narrowed her eyes at her sister, who playfully blew a kiss and waved. She just shook her head and turned back to her mother's questioning.

"His name is Jackson. It's not that serious," Noelle said finally.
"Liar! They've been dating for weeks! Almost months!" Shandra yelled from inside the pantry.
"Shut up, you!" Noelle yelled back.
"Uh, Miss Ma'am," Annabelle called Noelle's attention back to her. "Do you like him?"
"Yes, Ma'am. I do."
"Nola, look at me."

Noelle turned towards her mothers voice and looked into her eyes. Eyes so warm and maternal that looked just like her own.

"Are you happy, Baby?" Annabelle asked.

"Yeah...I really am," Noelle answered with a smile.

"Then that's all I need to know," Annabelle said, smiling back and cuffing Noelle's chin with her finger.

The two women pressed their foreheads together, sealing their moment with an unspoken understanding that only they needed.

"Well, I'm nosier than ya mama! What he look like?" Aunt Carolyn asked, breaking the silence in the kitchen.

The women all burst into laughter as Noelle described Jackson to them.

"He's tall, dark and fine as ever! He dresses nice and smells even better!" she said.

The ladies were all hooting and laughing when Noelle's grand-mother, Ernestine, finally walked into the kitchen, asking what was going on? They got her all caught up on what she missed, and she gave Noelle a nod of approval as she came in for a hug.

"He not comin' today, is he?" Ernestine quickly asked, lifting her brows.

"No, Ma'am," Noelle said.

"Whew! Okay, good," Ernestine said.

"Why you say that?" Noelle asked.

"Because, after the last time, don't you bring no mo' of yo' men 'round this family," Ernestine said.

"Mama, what is that supposed to mean?" Aunt Gladys asked.

"It means, as long as yo' daughter is in town ain't no man of Noelle's safe," Ernestine replied.

"Granny, she has who she wants now. I think I'm okay." Noelle said with a chuckle.

"Chil'e, please! If you don't 'member nothin' else I say, 'member this. Yesterday's tramp is today's tramp, and today's tramp is tomorrow's tramp. Don't you bring no man around her 'til after she's married off, and even then I wouldn't do it, hell!"

Everyone except Gladys laughed, and just then the kitchen door swung open and Marguerite walked in asking what everyone was laughing at?

"You," Ernestine said matter-of-factly as she walked over to the kitchen table.

"Well, it's nice to see you too, Grandma," Marguerite said as she went in to give her a hug and kiss.

"Girl, *we* don't do that shit. Now, move," Ernestine said as she waved her off.

"Grandma, why are you always so mean to me?" Marguerite asked, almost sounding hurt.

"You think I'm mean to you?"

"Yes, I do."

Ernestine looked at Marguerite quietly for a moment, pondering her question. She'd always been a straight shooter, so no sense in censoring the truth now.

"I don't like ya," she finally answered pointedly.

"Mama!" Gladys exclaimed.

"She asked," Ernestine said. "You're my gran'daughter, and for that fact, I love you. But, you got some ways about ya that I don't like. So, I don't fool with you. It's just that plain and simple."

Marguerite looked at her grandmother in silence for a minute and then just simply nodded. She didn't know what else to say. She went back to greeting the rest of the ladies in the kitchen, as if that would undo the awkward moment that had just occurred between her and Granny Ernestine.

"Hello, Noelle," Marguerite greeted her cousin.

"Marguerite, please don't feel obligated to speak to me every time you see me. It's really not necessary," Noelle replied, never looking up from the cutting board. Marguerite just shook her head.

"What about you, Shandy? Are *you* in a speaking mood today?" Marguerite asked.

Shandra stared blankly at her, blinking slowly and never saying a word. Marguerite rolled her eyes and shook her head before walking out of the kitchen, mumbling to herself as she went, "I see how this day is gonna go."

The family was all gathered around the table sharing in the feast prepared with love. Richard, Noelle's father, led the family in a prayer of thanks and her uncle, Eddie, Carolyn's husband, did the honor of carving the turkey. The dining room was filled with delicious aromas and hearty conversation. Every so often, a hush would fall around the table as everyone indulged in food that touched the soul. Then, the men would start excitedly discussing some play that happened during the game they watched earlier as they filled their plates with second helpings.

Another silence had fallen around the table once everyone was full and trying to decide if they should wait for dessert or not. Just then, Aunt Carolyn broke through with a question.

"So, Marguerite, have you guys set a date yet?" she asked, referring to Marguerite and Eric's pending nuptials.

He had accompanied her to yet another family dinner, against his better judgment. *Anything to keep the little woman happy*, he had told himself.

"We have actually," Marguerite replied. "It's set for January 25th."

"Oh! So soon?" Aunt Carolyn asked.

"Yeah, we didn't need a long engagement," she said.

Just then a light chuckle could be heard coming from Noelle, who sat across from the couple. Eric just eyed her curiously, but Marguerite asked what everyone else was thinking.

"What's so funny, Noelle?" she asked.

"Your wedding date. That's what's so funny," Noelle replied flatly.

"Wait. That wasn't *your* wedding date, was it, Nola?" Richie asked from the end of the table, staring at Marguerite and Eric through narrowed eyes.

"No, it wasn't," she said.

Noelle explained that the date chosen also happened to be the same date she caught them in bed together in the home she shared with Eric back when *she* was his wife. A few gasps and grumbles could be heard around the table, and then an awkward silence fell over the room as everyone waited to see where this conversation would lead.

"Really, Noelle? Are you ever gonna let that go?" Marguerite asked, annoyance present in her voice.

"And why the hell should I?" Noelle asked, a scowl forming on her face.

"Because it's been long enough!" Marguerite replied, rolling her eyes. "And because I'm sick of being the only one catching shit from you all these years."

"Sweetie, Eric catches just as much as you do. Don't feel special," Noelle said.

For a moment, Marguerite went quiet and broke eye contact. Noelle could see the wheels turning in her head and wondered where this drama was about to go. It honestly had been a long time coming and she was glad to finally get it all out. Marguerite looked at Noelle over the rim of her wine glass with a sneaky smirk. Noelle narrowed her eyes in suspicion at the gesture.

"*Sweetie*," Marguerite started, mocking Noelle's tone. "If you truly intend to carry that grudge for the rest of your life, then Eric and I ain't the only ones you need to be pissed at."

"What the hell are you talking about?" Noelle asked.

"Well, for starters, do you honestly think that the *one* time we *let* ourselves get caught by you, that that was the first time we had slept together?" Marguerite asked, propping her elbow on the table and resting her chin in her palm.

Noelle looked from Marguerite to Eric, shaking her head in bewilderment and trying to grasp what was being said to her, but found it hard to do.

"I can assure you, that *wasn't* the first time, *Sweetie*," Marguerite continued.

"So how many times was it, Eric?" Noelle asked her ex-husband, her hands clenched in fists under the table.

"Nola, can we please not do this right now?" Eric pleaded, stealing a glance at the many faces around the table.

"How many?!"

"I don't remember!"

Noelle fell back in her chair. She could feel her skin growing hot with rage, and her nails digging into the palms of her hands. She wondered how could he not remember? Had he cheated on her that often right under her nose? How could he do that to her? The questions rushed through her mind so rapidly, that Noelle couldn't even get them to come out of her mouth.

"Let me help you, cousin," Marguerite said, seeing Noelle's confusion. "How long would you say I lived with you guys, Babe? About six months?"

She turned to Eric for confirmation, and he nodded in agreement.

"Right, I was there for six months. But, I only kept my hands to myself for about the first two weeks," Marguerite said smugly with a shrug.

"Excuse me?!" Noelle exclaimed.

"Yup, and other people at this table knew about it. So, like I said, Eric and I ain't the only ones you should be pissed at, *Sweetie*," she added, tapping her engagement ring against her wine glass.

Noelle looked around the table at her supposed "loved" ones – people she trusted with her life.

"Who else knew?" Noelle asked, her jaw clenched tightly.

"Well, for one there's my mama. Your *favorite* aunt," Marguerite added sarcastically.

"What?!" Noelle shouted, looking down the table at her Aunt Gladys.

Aunt Gladys never looked up or made eye contact with Noelle. Marguerite went on to tell how her mother knew everything from the day the affair started up until the day Noelle left for good. She even mentioned how much of a gossiper her mother is known to be, especially when talking with her sister, Carolyn. So, it's very likely that she knew about the affair, as well. And if the two of them knew about it, there's no limit to who else they told. Thus, proving Marguerite's point that Noelle should be upset with more than just her and Eric.

Noelle looked at her aunt again, tears welling up in her eyes and her voice cracking as she tried to fight back her emotions. Aunt Gladys was like a second mother to Noelle, and Gladys loved her like she was her own daughter. When Noelle and Eric got married and moved to New York so he could attend Law School, Gladys would call every week just to check in and see how things were going.

Even when she asked Noelle to let Marguerite stay with her for a short while, the hope was that Noelle would be a positive influence on her cousin and set her on the right path. Seems like the only path she cared about was the one leading to Eric.

"How could you, Aunt Gladys? How could you know about this and not tell me?" Noelle asked, her voice filled with sadness.

"Noelle, you had everything," Gladys started, her eyes fixed on her niece's. "Everyone loved you and doted on you and treated you like you were special. And they treated my Marguerite like she was nothing. Sometimes less than nothing. It's every mother's wish for her daughter to find a man who will treat her right and take care of her, and my Marguerite found that."

"In somebody else's husband?!" Shandra shouted the question at her aunt.

"Look, if Eric was meant to be Noelle's, then none of *this* would've happened," Gladys snapped.

"Do you hear yourself, right now?!" Shandra fumed.

Gladys turned her attention back to Noelle. She apologized for the hurt and heartbreak her niece endured when her marriage fell apart, and tried to assure her that the man truly meant for her would find her someday.

"But Eric is the man for Marguerite, and we know that now. And it's just best that we all accept it," Gladys said matter-of-factly.

"So, let me get this straight," Annabelle piped up. "You betrayed *my* daughter and played a part in destroying her marriage, just so Marguerite could have a man?!"

"You know as well as I do, that a mother would do anything for her child's happiness," Gladys replied, cutting her eyes at her sister.

"Welp," Richard, Noelle's father, spoke for the first time.

He pushed his chair away from the table, got up and started walking away. Richie called after him and asked where he was going?

"I'm goin' out to my truck," Richard said calmly, and then turned his gaze towards Gladys, Marguerite and Eric. "And when I get back, I strongly advise the three of you not still be sittin' here."

Then he turned on his heels and walked out of the dining room. The sound of the front door opening and closing could be heard in the distance. Just then Granny Ernestine turned to the three of them and said pointedly, "Get out."

"What did you say, Mama?" Gladys asked.

"If I know my son-in-law like I believe I do, then he's comin' back in here with his pistol, and I for one, ain't gon' stop him," Ernestine said.

"That's exactly what's happenin'," Annabelle said, her eyes still staring daggers into her sister.

"While I don't blame him, I also don't want my house shot up on Thanksgivin'. So, I want you, ya tramp ass daughter and this trifilin' negro outta my house. Now."

Gladys looked at her mother wide-eyed – first in shock and then anger. She hated how they were always treated as the black sheep of the family, and she went on to say as much. However, her mother stood her ground and was unmoved.

"The way you acted and the way you treated this chil'e," Ernestine said, pointing at Noelle, "I know for a fact I ain't raise you like that. And 'til you take that shit back where ya got it from, you ain't no chil'e of mine. Now get ya ass up from my table and outta my house!"

The sound of clinking dishes and rattling silverware could be heard as Ernestine slammed her fist down on the table. Gladys, Marguerite and Eric all hurriedly got up at Granny's orders as they heard the front door open and close again. Gladys gave another half-hearted apology to Noelle before leaving, but it fell on deaf ears. Noelle sat silently for the longest time, barely breathing or even blinking.

Muted tears streamed one-by-one down her face as the reality of what she had just heard sunk in – one daggered word at a time. She could feel Shandra's hand rubbing her shoulder; could hear muffled voices around her, but not really making out what they were saying. Suddenly, she felt nauseous and her skin felt dirty. A dizziness started in her head, and she thought for sure she would faint.

Noelle slowly closed her eyes and took four deep breaths, trying to collect herself. She rotated her neck left to right and could hear the crack of her vertebrae echoing in her ears. She finally unclenched her fists beneath the table and wiggled her fingers to get the blood flowing again.

Then her eyelids flew open and she stared into the spaces once occupied by her traitorous cousin, aunt and ex-husband. Then her eyes slowly surveyed the faces of her other relatives seated at the table. Faces she had seen all her life, but today she had no idea who these people were...and right now, she hated all of them. Noelle got up from the table and walked out of her grandmother's house, never uttering a single word.

Nine

Noelle flipped lazily through the pages of a *Macy's* catalog promoting some holiday sales. She had no intentions of actually going shopping, but just needed something to pass the time while her coffee brewed. The aroma of French vanilla-flavored coffee beans filled her kitchen. The sound of the slow drip hitting the inside of the glass coffee pot did its best to drown out the incessant buzzing of her cellphone.

Since walking out on Thanksgiving dinner at her Grandmother's house, Noelle hadn't spoken a single word to anyone in her family. Everyone from her parents and siblings to her grandmother had been calling constantly. Even her Aunt Gladys had called and sent texts trying to reach out, but to no avail. Noelle had officially cut off every relative she had.

After learning the whole truth of how Marguerite's betrayal wasn't just her cross to bear alone, but that other family members had known all along, as well; it was all too much for Noelle to take. Knowing that the same people who professed to love her all her life had also played a role in destroying that same life, and not being sure of who, if anyone, was innocent in all of this just made Noelle sick to her stomach. The lies and the hurt of it all was the last straw, and Noelle had nothing left in her to be the bigger person, or to put the family first.

"Fuck the family," she mumbled to herself as she poured the piping hot coffee into a yellow porcelain mug.

She brought it to her lips, inhaling the scent and enjoying the warmth of the steam on her face. The serenity of the moment was interrupted by the familiar buzzing of her phone against the glass tabletop. Noelle rolled her eyes when she saw her brother's name flashing across the screen. She grabbed the catalog off the table, and took it and her coffee to the sofa.

Noelle had spent the last two days in the house, going from the sofa to the recliner to her bed and back to the sofa again. A variety of pajamas, fuzzy footies and a cozy cardigan had been her wardrobe of choice as she relaxed and ignored the world. She was snuggled under her favorite purple fleece throw and watching a movie when she heard the doorbell. The sound made her jump as she wasn't expecting any visitors.

From her seat on the sofa, Noelle peeked through the partially opened curtains covering the front window. She could see her sister, Shandra, on the front porch.

"Hmph," Noelle grunted and turned her attention back to the television.

She pulled the blanket up to cover herself more and rested her chin on her fist, getting more comfortable. Shandra rang the bell and knocked on the door several more times. She even called Noelle's name when she spotted her through the window. Noelle never turned towards the door or her sister and never left her seat on the couch.

"Noelle! Noelle, I know you hear me!" Shandra shouted, now knocking on the window. "Noelle! Seriously?!"

Shandra had called Noelle every day, multiple times a day since Thursday, but never got a response. She had sent multiple text messages, and even went as far as an email or two. They all went unanswered. Shandra and Noelle talked all the time, probably more often than people thought to be normal. So, this wall of silence Noelle had erected was something Shandra did not know how to deal with. She rang and knocked and knocked and rang, but got nothing.

"Noelle!" Shandra yelled at the window, her voice cracking with emotion.

She pressed her head against the screen door, trying to get her breathing and emotions under control as tears welled up in her eyes. Being shut out like this was breaking her heart with each passing second. Shandra dejectedly left Noelle's porch after her fifteen-minute assault on the door, doorbell and window yielded no results. She was walking back to her car parked in the driveway when she spotted a fire engine backing into the garage of the firehouse down the street from Noelle's house.

Shandra remembered that was the station where Jackson and Aundre worked, and she decided now was the time to call for reinforcements. She walked up to the open door of the firehouse and spotted Aundre and another fireman unloading equipment from the truck. Coming here was her last ditch effort to get Noelle's attention somehow.

"Dre," Shandra called out, her voice still cracking and sounding strained.

Aundre looked around the open door of the firetruck and spotted Shandra. At first he smiled, until he noticed her tear-stained face and immediately became worried. He rushed to her side to see what was wrong.

"Is Jackson here?" Shandra asked, sniffling and wiping away tears.
"Yeah, he's upstairs. Bae, what's wrong?" Aundre asked, cupping her face in his hand.

"Can you get him, please?" she asked.

"Is everything okay?"

"No."

Aundre immediately pulled out his cellphone and called Jackson, telling him that a crying Shandra was downstairs asking for him. Before Aundre could finish delivering his message, Jackson was coming down the steps in a rush. He frantically asked Shandra what was wrong and if Noelle was okay. She told him about how distant and unresponsive Noelle was being to everyone. So, she couldn't honestly say for sure if her sister was okay or not.

"Did something happen? Does she usually get like this?" Jackson asked, trying to understand further.

"No, she's never done this before," Shandra replied.

"So what caused it?"

"Family drama. It's a long story, but now she's not even talking to *me*! That isn't like her, at all!"

Jackson paused for a moment, taking in everything Shandra had said, and even reading between the lines of what she *didn't* say. He tried to assure her that if Noelle needed some space to deal with whatever was going on, then respect that. Pressing her to talk or see people when she's not in the mood will only make things worse for everybody.

"Have you talked to her at all?" Aundre asked Jackson.

"Not since before the holiday. Figured she'd be spending time with the family. Didn't want to impose," Jackson replied.

"A lot of good that did," Shandra said sarcastically with a sniffle.

"I'm sure, besides being a little pissed off, she's fine," Jackson said, rubbing Shandra's arm for comfort.

"Can you do me a favor, then?" Shandra asked.

"Of course."

"Can *you* try getting in touch with her? Just like a well-being check or something? As far as everything goes, you're an innocent party in all of this. She may actually talk to *you*."

Jackson promised Shandra he would check on Noelle and give her any update he had. She thanked him and apologized for dragging him into their family drama, but he told her no apology was necessary. He left her and Aundre alone and headed back upstairs to the loft, but paused for a moment in the stairwell to make a quick phone call.

"Hey, TJ. It's Jackson," he said after his friend, a local Houston police officer, picked up on the second ring.

"Hey Jack! How's it going?" TJ greeted cheerfully through the receiver.

"I'm good, man. Can't complain. Look, I need a favor. Off the books."

"I'm listening."

Jackson yanked up the zipper on his gray Adidas track jacket as he let out a heavy sigh. His shift at the firehouse had just ended and he was changing out of his uniform to head home for his two days off. He slipped on his hi-top Adidas sneakers, and a gray and black Memphis Grizzlies fitted cap, letting out an exasperated sigh with each motion. His friend TJ rode by Noelle's house to do a "sneak & peek," as he called it, to check on her per Jackson's request. As he rolled by, he caught a glimpse of her coming out to check the mail and wave at a neighbor. TJ advised Jackson that she looked fine and well as far as he could see and felt no cause for concern.

"What'd you do?" TJ had asked when he called back.

"Now why would you assume I did something?" Jackson asked, sounding mildly offended.

"Why else would I be checking on her instead of you, then?"

"Because well-being checks are your job, dude!"

"Not off the books, they ain't!"

Jackson gave TJ the background story, as far as he knew, of what was going on between Noelle and her family, and how he had wanted to make sure she was, in fact, okay without him invading her space to do so. He had fully intended to let TJ's status report be satisfactory for him, and even assured Shandra of the same when he texted her an update. Yet, right now something was stirring inside of Jackson that he was struggling to ignore. He even shook his head a few times like he was trying to toss those nagging thoughts from his mind. It wasn't working, though.

Jackson snatched up his duffle bag from the metal bench and slammed his locker shut, his frustration very obvious. So much so that Aundre had to comment on it.

"You good, bruh?" Aundre asked as he finished buttoning his maroon silk dress shirt.

"Huh?...Oh, yeah. I'm aight," Jackson replied absentmindedly.

"Go check on her, Man," Aundre said, adjusting the cuffs of his shirt and never looking at Jackson.

"I don't need to. TJ already checked."

"Jackson."

"What? He said she's fine."

"Jackson."

"What, Man?!"

Aundre finally turned to look his friend in the eyes. He stepped forward and extended his hand. He and Jackson dapped and pulled each other into an embrace. Jackson pulled out of their hug first but Aundre didn't release his hand, which made Jackson look at him questioningly.

"Go check on your lady, Bruh," Aundre commanded. "*Do not* wait for her to call you. If she's as stubborn as Shandy, then I doubt she will call you with her problems, but that *does not* mean she doesn't need you right now. So, go."

Jackson knew he was right and didn't even bother arguing, plus he knew it would bug him incessantly until he laid eyes on Noelle for himself. He assured Aundre he would check on her as soon as possible and hoped he'd have an easier time than her family when trying to do so.

"Where the hell are you going dressed like Rico Suave, anyway?" Jackson asked with a chuckle as he headed towards the doorway of the locker room.

"Shut up! I got a date," Aundre said with a huge grin.

"A *date*? With *who*?" Jackson asked, raising a curious eyebrow.

"Shandy," said Aundre, still grinning.

"Nice!" Jackson exclaimed and dapped up Aundre one last time before heading out.

Jackson stood on Noelle's porch completely drawing a blank on how he would explain just popping up at her house unannounced. He knew bringing up her family would be a touchy subject, but without them he had nothing. *Hopefully I won't have to explain this stupid shit,* he thought to himself as his hand hovered over the doorbell. Jackson thought the chime of it might be too much and opted to just knock.

*Knock. Knock...*Silence. *Knock. Knock. Knock...*Silence.

Jackson glanced over at the living room window to his left and could see the lamp light shining through and could even slightly hear the television. Just then it clicked. This is what she's been doing for days to everybody else. *She probably just thinks it's her family bugging her again,* he thought. Taking a deep breath, Jackson decided to risk revealing his identity like some lovestruck superhero.

"Noelle," Jackson called through the closed door. Suddenly, he could no longer hear the television. He knocked lightly again and said, "Noelle, baby it's me...It's Jackson."

At the sound of his voice, Noelle sat up on the sofa and stared at the door. Was it really him? If so, what was he doing here? How did he know she wanted to see him? She squinted her eyes in the door's direction, as if that would help her hear better or answer any of her questions.

Noelle got up and hesitantly walked towards the door and could instantly feel his heat on her skin like he was standing next to her. She undid the locks with a shaky hand and pulled open the door to see Jackson standing just outside the screen door. He smiled gently at the sight of her, but Noelle stood there straight-faced and silent, blinking slowly.

"Hey, Gorgeous," Jackson greeted her warmly. "How are you?"

Noelle didn't respond, just stared and blinked. The smile faded from Jackson's face and a frown of concern replaced it.

"Noe, are you okay?" he asked softly, frown lines marring his forehead.

That one simple question was like a stone crashing into a stained-glass window, shattering the picture-perfect image into infinite shards. Tears welled up in Noelle's eyes. Her body began to tremble. The rigid resolve she had worn like armor the last few days fell like a house of cards. Finally, Noelle bursts into sobs as she stood there silently holding the door open. Jackson's eyes widened and he immediately reached for the knob of the screen door, but it was locked.

"Noe, baby please unlock the door," Jackson said frantically as he tugged on the knob.

Noelle covered her face with her hands as the sobs continued, which only made Jackson more persistent. He knocked rapidly on the glass to get her attention, which worked, surprisingly. Their eyes met, and Noelle saw the pleading and worry on Jackson's face.

"Baby, please. Please, unlock this. Let me in, Baby," Jackson coaxed, his hands splayed on the glass.

With a trembling hand, Noelle turned the lock on the screen door and Jackson immediately rushed in. He pulled her into his arms with such force it made her gasp, but the warmth of his chest pressed against her tear-soaked face and his muscular arms draped tightly around her entire upper body gave Noelle all the security she needed. Security to shed her defenses and allow herself to live in her emotions freely and honestly.

The moment Noelle walked out of her Grandmother's house on Thanksgiving, she had adamantly refused to allow any emotions besides rage and hatred to exist inside of her. But, at this moment in Jackson's arms, Noelle gave herself permission to break. And break she did. He could feel Noelle's body completely collapse against him, nearly sinking from the weight of all the emotions she had been holding in.

The harder she cried, the tighter he held her, cupping the back of her head with his hand and planting soothing kisses atop her head while softly whispering, "It's okay. I'm here," over and over. Then Jackson scooped her up, kicked the door closed and carried her over to the sofa. He sat down, cradling Noelle in his lap and rocked her gently. He never asked a question or said a word besides, "It's okay. I'm here."

She didn't need words. She didn't need demands for her time and energy. She just needed to be free to fall apart, without question or judgment and to feel safe enough to do so. And that's exactly what Jackson was giving her in that moment – freedom and safety. Something Noelle never had until now.

They sat in silence as Noelle's tears slowed and her breathing calmed. Jackson caressed her back and shoulders as she lay nestled in his lap. Their rhythmic breathing and Noelle's soft sniffles were the only sounds around them in the comforting silence.

"I'm sorry," Noelle finally said as she sat up and wiped the tears from her face.

"You have nothing to apologize for," Jackson said calmly as he brushed loose strands of hair from her face.

"I'm sure you don't want to see me being an emotional wreck," she said.

Jackson cuffed her chin and turned her face towards his.

"I want to see you in every form you come in," he said reassuringly. "I'm honored to be your safe space right now. Don't apologize. You needed to get that out, and I'm glad I could be here for you while you did."

Noelle suddenly realized she didn't know why Jackson had randomly arrived on her doorstep without calling or texting first. He told her about Shandra coming to the firehouse to ask that he check in on her since she was giving the family the cold shoulder. Noelle rolled her eyes, annoyed with her sister for dragging him into their mess.

"I'm sorry she bothered you with this," Noelle said, shaking her head and rubbing her eyes.

"I'm not," Jackson said matter-of-factly.

"You have much better things to do and places to be than here getting my snot and tears on you," she said jokingly.

"Noelle, let me be here for you. It's okay, I promise," he whispered against her neck as he planted soft kisses along her pulse.

Noelle melted under his soft touch and even softer lips. She had to admit it felt damn good to shed her emotional armor with someone, even if it scared her a little.

"Noelle?" Jackson called to her.

"Yeah?" she replied in a light whisper, fighting back a second wave of tears.

"Can I take care of you?"

"Yes, you can."

Jackson told her to go pack a bag because he was whisking her away for a few days. Since he had the next two days off and she was taking time off, as well, now seemed like the perfect time. Not to mention, he knew if she stayed home her family would not leave her be like she so obviously wanted. So, Jackson offered to take Noelle on an impromptu getaway where he could continue his care for her and she could be free to deal with her emotions however she chose.

He tempted her with promises of home cooked meals, jacuzzi-style bubble baths and endless cuddles and massages for the next two days – an offer she certainly could not refuse. Noelle mustered up the energy to dart upstairs and pack her bags. These were not the ideal circumstances she had hoped for on their first getaway together, but she was going to do everything in her power to enjoy it. This was one thing she would not allow her family drama, or Eric and Marguerite's evil ways to ruin for her.

Noelle rifled through the drawers to grab socks, underwear and pajamas, but as she went to put them inside her duffle bag, she paused for a second. *If I'm lucky, maybe I won't even need pjs*, she snickered at the thought then shoved the items in her bag. She darted into the bathroom to wrangle some toiletries to take with her, but grimaced at her reflection in the mirror above the sink. Her eyes were so puffy and red and her nose was still running a little from her earlier crying spell. She splashed some cold water on her face trying to wash away the salty streaks down her cheeks and headed back to her bedroom to finish packing.

While waiting for Noelle to come back down, Jackson went to the kitchen to get himself some water. As he reached for the door handle of the refrigerator, he noticed several small cards posted on the front. He lifted the flap of one and read the message inside. He gave a subtle nod as he lifted the flap on another and read that one. He exhaled a sigh, eyeing the seven cards adorning the door of the refrigerator and gave another slight nod before pulling it open and grabbing a bottle of water.

Jackson was taking a sip when he heard Noelle bopping down the stairs. He came out of the kitchen to meet her in the living room. He saw the faint glint of happiness in her eyes as she swung her duffle bag next to her leg. He flashed a quick smile and leaned in to kiss her lightly on the lips before taking the bag from her hand.

"Somebody's popular, I see," Jackson said coyly.
"What do you mean?" Noelle asked, frowning slightly.
"The cards on the fridge," he said, pointing towards the kitchen.
"Oh, yeah!" she replied in a perky tone.

Noelle explained that she had been receiving floral arrangements delivered to the shop like clockwork every Thursday for the last few weeks. Every bouquet was different and no two cards were ever the same. She gushed about how sweet the words were and how much the gift of flowers, "Just Because," always made her smile.

"So, who sent them? Do you know?" Jackson asked, as he helped with her coat.

"No," Noelle said, shaking her head. "There was never a signature on the cards and the deliveries were sent anonymously."

"Interesting," he said quietly.

"Everybody teased me about it being some secret admirer, but I hated not knowing who it was," she said with a pout.

Jackson held the front door open so Noelle could walk through it, and just as she passed him to step out on the porch, he whispered behind her.

"Psst," Jackson beckoned.

"Yeesss," Noelle sang as she turned to face him.

"The secret's out," he whispered and winked at her.

"Wait! What?!" she exclaimed in shock. "*You*?!"

"Why do you sound so surprised?"

"Well, I just mean that we've been seeing each other for a while now. Why keep sending flowers after you've already gotten the girl?"

"So, I can *keep* the girl."

Noelle exhaled a laugh as she slid into the passenger seat of Jackson's truck. He leaned in and kissed her sweetly on the lips, before closing the door and going around to the driver's side.

Ten

Jackson pulled his black Ford F-250 pickup truck into the attached garage of his two-story townhome. He grabbed Noelle's rose pink leather Michael Kors duffle bag off the backseat and went around to the passenger side to help her out of the truck. The pair walked to the door leading into the house and stepped inside just as the garage door came down, bathing the space in darkness.

He flipped on the hall light as they removed their shoes. The cool white and gray marble tiled floor greeted the bottoms of Noelle's sock-covered feet. Jackson hung his car keys on the brass hook embedded in the wall, then took her hand again, guiding her further into the house.

The short hallway led into a miniature chef's kitchen, with oak cabinets and ceramic countertops. An island with a sink and barstool seating stood in the center surrounded by stainless steel appliances. A glass-top kitchen table with maroon-colored plush cushioned chairs sat nestled next to the bay window looking out into the backyard.

Stepping out of the kitchen into the foyer leading to the front of the house, Jackson turned to Noelle, who offered up a half smile as their eyes met.

"Welcome to my home, Babe," Jackson said as he brushed away the

"

hair from Noelle's forehead to place a soft kiss there. "As promised, I'm going to take good care of you the next few days."

He led her upstairs, bringing them to a plush carpeted landing. Two guest rooms and a bathroom faced the staircase and the master bedroom was the first door to the left of the stairs. They walked into Jackson's bedroom and Noelle was immediately impressed. There was a black wrought iron, king-size, four-poster bed in the center of the room with black cotton sheets and a black and silver comforter covering the mattress.

To the left was a long dresser with black finish and wrought iron handles on the six drawers. A large mirror and vast collection of cologne bottles, jewelry and other trinkets were scattered on top. A 52-inch flat screen TV hung on the wall in front of the bed and a high back charcoal gray recliner with a small end-table sat in the corner to the right of the bed. Between the room's décor and the soft, lush speckled carpet beneath her feet, Noelle could truly appreciate Jackson's sense of style.

Jackson sat down Noelle's bag on the leather bench at the foot of the bed before disappearing around a short corner. Giving in to her curiosity, Noelle followed and was instantly speechless. Jackson's master bathroom had both a standing shower with glass doors and a waterfall shower head and a separate raised jacuzzi bathtub. There was also a wall-length mirror and double basin sink with granite countertop that matched the granite walls and floors of the shower and border of the bathtub. After only seeing three rooms so far, Noelle couldn't wait to see what the rest of Jackson's home had to offer.

"I'm going to run you a hot bath," Jackson's deep voice penetrated Noelle's thoughts. "I have some candles under the sink. Light whichever ones you like. I want you to fully relax and get comfortable."

"Thank you, Jackson," Noelle said with a full smile this time.

"You're welcome, Beautiful."

With the bathroom now bathed in the soft glow and sweet fragrance of cardamom and vanilla candles, Noelle lowered herself into the hot bubble bath Jackson had prepared. The jacuzzi jets were pulsating beneath the water – their light humming played a soothing rhythm that calmed her senses. The warm water and lathery suds covered Noelle all the way up to her collarbone as she submerged her tired body. She rested her head against the foam cushion affixed to the back of the tub and slowly closed her eyes. *Peace at last*, she thought.

Jackson brought the wooden spoon covered in red sauce up to his mouth to taste his concoction. He had gone down to make dinner for the two of them while Noelle enjoyed her bath. Soft R&B played throughout the kitchen from the Bluetooth speaker on the counter and Jackson moved expertly around the stove. Tonight he was crafting his special version of chicken marsala with wild rice and sautéed asparagus. This was his first time cooking for Noelle, and he wanted to make something impressive.

Jackson was in the middle of chopping some red onion and mushrooms when his phone chimed with a text notification. It was from Noelle.

Hey, Lovey. Sorry to bug you. I need your help with something really quick, please?

He sent a short reply saying he was on his way, turned the sauce down to a simmer and washed his hands before heading out of the kitchen and up the stairs. He walked into his bedroom, but didn't see Noelle anywhere.

"Noe?" he called out to her, looking around the room.

"I'm in here!" Noelle replied from the bathroom.

Jackson walked towards the cracked bathroom door where slivers of candlelight peeked out. He lightly knocked before pushing open the door with his fingertips.

"Hey, Baby. What did you need help...with?" Jackson's voice trailed off as he entered the bathroom and laid eyes on Noelle smirking in the tub.

He exhaled a light chuckle as he shyly dropped his gaze to the floor.

"What's wrong, Jackson?" Noelle asked in a sultry tone.

"Uh...nothing's wrong. N-Nothing at all," Jackson stammered, still averting his gaze.

"Are you sure?" she pressed, still smirking.

"Very. Umm...W-What did you need help with, Babe?" he asked, trying hard to stay on topic.

"You have to come here first," she beckoned.

Jackson looked in the mirror above the sink and caught Noelle's reflection over his left shoulder. He could see the sneaky flirty-ness in her eyes and devilish grin on her face following what she'd said. He slowly licked his lips as a matching smile crept across his face and he exhaled another light chuckle. He turned on his heels and walked slowly, yet purposefully, over to Noelle wading beneath the sudsy water.

Jackson came to stand next to the tub, slipping his hands into his pockets and Noelle welcomed the opportunity to drink in every inch of him. The way his chocolate skin seemed to glow and glisten in the candlelight. The way his black sweatpants fit his muscular legs and thighs and sat low on his hips. How his gray tank top clung tightly to every inch of his torso as his perfect pecs rose and fell with each breath. The definition in his strong arms decorated with pulsating veins was proof positive of the powerful, red blooded male he was through and through.

Noelle dragged her gaze along the entire length of his body – from his large feet up to his long legs, up to his narrow waist, up to his wide chest, up to his thick neck, up to his lush beard covering his strong jawline and framing his high cheekbones. Then their eyes met, and the silence between them became so loud it made Noelle's ears ring and heart race. She inhaled one deep breath, taking in the aromatic cocktail of scented candles, eucalyptus bubble bath and Jackson's Givenchy cologne. She held that one breath for what felt like an eternity.

"What did you need, Baby?" Jackson repeated softly, breaking the silence.

"It requires you to get in the tub first," Noelle exhaled her reply, never breaking eye contact.

"Get in the tub?" he asked with a raised eyebrow.

"Yes. Get *in* the tub."

"You sure 'bout that?"

"Positive."

"Okay."

Jackson slid his tank top up his stomach and chest at a torturous pace before finally pulling it over his head. Then he slipped his fingers into the waistband of his sweatpants and pushed them down to his ankles just as slowly. He stepped out of his pants and socks, leaving on nothing but his boxers. Jackson looked into Noelle's eyes again for reassurance and she sensually licked her full lips. That was all he needed. He took his boxers off and stepped into the jacuzzi, sitting on the seat jutting out of the tub's wall at the opposite end facing Noelle.

"If all you wanted was some company," Jackson started, trying to hide a half grin.

His words were cut short when Noelle shifted from her position and floated towards him, her brown eyes intensely fixed on his dark hazel ones. When she got to him, she reached out beneath the water and placed her hands on his abs. She caressed her way up his chest, with her perfectly manicured hands emerging from beneath the sudsy water as they traveled up. She stood between Jackson's legs and gripped his firm shoulders.

Jackson licked and tucked his bottom lip under his teeth as he anxiously anticipated Noelle's next move. She cupped his face in her wet hands as she brought their lips together. The kiss was hungry and animalistic – almost feral. Jackson's hands clasped on to Noelle's ribs and waist tightly as their kiss intensified. She massaged the nape of his neck and ran her fingers through his short hair as she feasted on his mouth.

Noelle straddled Jackson on the jacuzzi seat. Her curvaceous torso rose out of the water with bubbles spread across her plump breasts and trailing down her flat stomach and hips – hips that disappeared beneath the water again as she lowered herself onto him. Jackson inhaled sharply against her mouth when he felt the tip of his manhood against her core. His grip on her waist tightened even more the further he felt himself slip inside of her.

Noelle's hips created an erotic rhythm as they moved back and forth...up and down...in slow sensuous circles. The bath water splashed against them in a tantric tidal wave with every motion.

"Sssshit, Baby," Jackson hissed as his eyes rolled back.

His large hands cupped her heavy breasts, stroking her nipples with the pad of his thumb. Noelle whimpered and moaned with every touch and thrust. She pressed her forehead to his and gripped his shoulders tighter as she moved her hips faster against him. Noelle could feel the intense rush of ecstasy building up inside of her, ready to explode.

Jackson reached up and grabbed Noelle's throat, pressing his fingers and thumb firmly against the sides.

"Look at me, Baby," Jackson commanded, his voice heavy with lust.

Noelle blinked open her eyes and they were wild and full of passion. Just what Jackson wanted.

"Cum for me," he demanded breathily against her lips.

Noelle's whimpers and cries grew louder. He could feel the grip of her thighs and walls tightening around every inch of him and it drove him crazy. Jackson grabbed Noelle's hip with his other hand, rocking and pulling her back and forth even faster, making her moan even louder.

"Cum for me, Baby," Jackson encouraged.

Noelle dug her nails into his shoulder and let out a throaty scream as an earth-shaking orgasm rocked her body from the inside out.

"That's it. That's my baby," he coaxed as he felt Noelle's body quake against him.

Jackson thrusted deeper inside of her, making sure he felt every part of her release as he found his own. His fingertips pressed hard into her hip and he growled against her neck as he reached his peak.

"Oh, my God," Noelle exhaled as she collapsed against Jackson, who let out an exhausted chuckle.

Jackson stroked Noelle's back lightly as they fought to catch their breath. He cradled her close as they sat in the tub riding out the last waves of erotic euphoria they had just created.

Eleven

Noelle could hear the distinct clinking of wine glasses coming from the kitchen. She was sitting on Jackson's sofa with her legs tucked under her and wearing one of his Houston Fire Department sweatshirts. After their hot and steamy bath time tryst, they had a romantic candle lit dinner prepared by Jackson's own hands.

"I had no idea you were such a good cook, sir," Noelle had complimented.

"Well, I am a fireman. It kinda comes with the territory," Jackson had said playfully.

Now Noelle was relaxing on the coffee-colored camel suede sofa in Jackson's living room, watching the flames dance inside the electric fireplace. She was laying a rust-colored throw blanket across her bare legs when Jackson came into the room carrying two half-filled glasses of Cabernet. He was shirtless and barefoot with his black sweatpants sitting low on his hips. Noelle licked her lips at the enticing sight of his "V" cuts peeking past the waistband.

Jackson handed her a glass before joining her on the sofa. For a while they just sat and sipped in silence, basking in the comfort of each other's company. Noelle was lightly stroking Jackson's shoulder with her fingertips as he rested his hand on her thigh. The fireplace hummed and cast shadows throughout the room, while bathing them in amber light that made them glow in the dark.

Hesitantly, Noelle decided to break the soothing silence between them.

"So," she started softly. "Aren't you gonna ask?"

"Didn't think I needed to," Jackson replied simply, taking a sip of wine.

"Why not?" she wondered, tilting her head slightly.

"Because if it was something more I needed to know or you wanted to share, then you'd tell me," he said calmly. "What I *do* know is that someone or something hurt you and you needed comfort. That was enough for me."

Noelle smiled at Jackson's sweet words because she knew he meant every one. All he wanted to do was be there for her during one of the most difficult moments of her life, and that meant the world to her. To truly feel safe in the hands of someone else, especially a man, was something Noelle thought she'd never experience again. But, with Jackson, all she wanted to do was strip away all her defenses and be completely vulnerable.

Hell, she had cried and snotted in front of him just a few hours ago! If that's not raw, unfiltered vulnerability, then what is?

"Someone did hurt me," Noelle confessed quietly, "Actually, in light of current events, it turns out there was a whole entourage involved."

Jackson leaned forward and sat his wine glass on the coffee table. He turned to face Noelle, who was now looking down at the burgundy liquid dancing inside the glass she held in trembling hands. He cupped her hands inside of his own and placed a kiss on her forehead.

"Noelle, it's okay," Jackson said comfortingly. "You don't have to tell me, if it's too much."

"No, no. It's not too much," Noelle replied, swiping a lone tear from her cheek.

After a ragged deep breath, Noelle told Jackson the sordid tale of her once happy and now dissolved marriage to Eric Pastor. She told him everything from their puppy-love fueled college years, to marrying young, to them moving to New York and chasing Eric's dreams of being a NYU law student. Then Noelle shared the painful details of his infidelity committed in the home they shared, and how it was with her own cousin.

Jackson sat quietly, giving Noelle all the time she needed to open up to him about the pain she had endured. Though he never uttered a word, Jackson was boiling inside at the thought of any man hurting Noelle, but the fact that it was her husband just made his internal rage go red hot. When she arrived at the details of what happened with her family at Thanksgiving dinner a few days ago, Jackson whipped his head around in disbelief.

"Wait!" Jackson exclaimed, waving his hands to halt Noelle's story. "You mean other people in your family knew about the affair and everything?!"

"Yep," Noelle said flatly, never making eye contact with him.

Jackson cuffed her chin with his finger, lifting her head. As their eyes met, he leaned forward and kissed her softly on one cheek and then the other before placing one on her lips. That kiss said to Noelle that everything is and will be okay. It said that her pain was real and valid, but it also let her know that she was safe from ever feeling such pain and betrayal again. That kiss said Jackson took pride in being trusted with not only Noelle's body, but with her heart. He had every intention of handling both with care and nothing less. Yes, that one kiss spoke volumes that words couldn't reach.

Jackson grabbed the wine glass from Noelle's hands and sat it on the coffee table next to his own. He pulled the fleece throw off her legs, slowly dragging the soft material across her bare thighs and leaving a trail of goosebumps along every inch of her skin. He cupped her face with one hand and grabbed her waist with the other as he used his body weight to lean her backwards, laying her flat on the sofa.

Instinctively, Noelle brought her legs up and wrapped them around Jackson's waist just as their lips met again for a more intense, passionate kiss. Their tongues danced to the rhythm of their moans and heavy breathing. Noelle's hands gripped Jackson's shoulder blades and her thighs tightened around him when she felt his strong fingertips pressing into her flesh.

Jackson nibbled at the corner of Noelle's lip, then trailed kisses along her jawline and down her neck. Her sharp intake of breath and soft whimpers were just more kindling on the lustful fire burning inside him, and he couldn't resist his aching need to be inside of her. He pulled away from her embrace just long enough to slide his sweatpants down. Noelle's brown eyes darkened with desire in the hearth light as she took in the sight of Jackson's immaculate naked form.

He kissed his way up her right leg, from calf to inner thigh to her precious center. Noelle could feel his warm breath and wet tongue as Jackson began to devour her. She stretched her arms above her head and dug her nails into the arm of the couch. Jackson moaned his satisfaction at the taste of her on his lips. He held her hips tightly, holding her hostage to the intensity of the orgasm building up inside her.

"Jackson!" Noelle cried out as spasms of ecstasy coursed through her core.

The sounds of Noelle peaking drove Jackson crazy. He flicked his tongue against her bud faster and harder, sending her writhing over the edge. Noelle grabbed Jackson's head with shaky hands as her cries of passion grew louder. She wanted to beg him to stop because she couldn't take it, but she also prayed he never would because it felt so damn good.

Jackson moved his way up Noelle's body, sliding the sweatshirt up inch-by-inch, kissing every piece of skin he revealed. He pushed the shirt over Noelle's head, leaving her nakedness to match his own. Their bodies were bathed in the amber light of the embers, making them glow in the dimness. Jackson slid inside of Noelle just as their lips met, and she raked her nails across his muscular back as his hips rocked back and forth.

A soundtrack of their sensuous panting and moaning, and low humming of the fireplace filled the room as Noelle and Jackson imprinted themselves on the sofa, melting into each other with every stroke.

◇ ◇ ◇ ◇ ◇ ◇

The faint scent of maple bacon and hazelnut coffee invaded Jackson's nostrils as he inhaled deeply and stretched his limbs, rousing himself awake. He swiped his hand across the space next to him in bed and noticed it was empty.

"Hmmm," he groaned in the quiet room as his eyes tried to focus.

Jackson rolled to the edge of the bed and swung his legs over the side, planting his feet on the floor. He grabbed a pair of green and black plaid pajama pants from the bench at the foot of the bed and lazily slipped them on before walking out of the bedroom. He followed the delicious smells filling his home, finding his way to the kitchen. What he saw made his heart smile.

Noelle was standing at the island whisking away at a bowl of cracked eggs – the motion made her butt wiggle a little beneath the oversized t-shirt, and Jackson couldn't help but stare. The bacon was sizzling on the stove, the coffeemaker was brewing and the Bluetooth speaker was blasting "Saturday Love" by Alexander O'Neal and Cherrelle. The entire scene was pure bliss to Jackson.

He walked up behind Noelle, pressing his pelvis against her backside as he kissed the nape of her neck. Noelle gasped and giggled lightly. She had come to love how Jackson touched her in any way. It always felt so firm, yet gentle; masculine, yet sensual. Noelle bit her bottom lip as Jackson planted feather-light kisses along the side of her neck up to her ear.

"Good morning, Gorgeous," Jackson whispered as he kissed her ear-lobe.

"Good morning, Handsome," Noelle greeted flirtatiously as she added shredded cheese and chopped spinach to the bowl of eggs.

"What do we have here?" he asked, peeking over her shoulder into the bowl.

"I'm making veggie omelets for breakfast," she said cheerfully.

"Veggie omelets?"

"Yup!"

"With bacon on the side?"

"Yeah. It's called a *balanced* meal for a reason."

Jackson laughed and placed another quick kiss on top of Noelle's head before making his way to the refrigerator to get some water. Noelle finished cooking, and joined him at the kitchen table to enjoy their breakfast in front of the large bay window. The sunlight shone beautifully through the blinds and swept brightly across the table. For a short while, they ate quietly as 90's R&B continued to play throughout the kitchen.

After taking a sip of his coffee, Jackson was the first to speak.

"Noe, I just wanted to say thank you," he started.

"You're welcome! Wait, what are you thanking me for, exactly?" Noelle asked with a light chuckle.

"For breakfast, for sure," Jackson said with a smile. "But, also for opening up to me last night. You shared something very personal with me when you didn't have to, and I appreciate you for trusting me with...*you*."

Noelle smiled and reached across the table to touch Jackson's arm. She thanked him for bringing her to his home and taking such good care of her, especially when she was dealing with so much. Just being able to relax and hide away, even for a little while was exactly what Noelle needed and Jackson provided that without hesitation. Over the last few hours, they had shared many intimate moments, on a variety of levels, and with each one Jackson had handled Noelle with such tenderness. It truly made her heart melt when she thought about it.

"I just want you to know that you're not alone in your pain from betrayal," Jackson continued.

"How do you mean?" Noelle asked with a furrowed brow.

"I went through something similar," he said quietly.

"Really?" she asked in surprise.

"Yeah. It's why I left Memphis, honestly."

Memphis, TN - 2016...

Back in Memphis, Jackson had it all. He was fresh out of the Firefighter Academy and managed to land a job at one of the firehouses in his childhood neighborhood. Jackson even had a fiancée, Stacey, who he had proposed to at his graduation party. To him, life was perfect and everything was falling into place.

He had been working at the firehouse for about nine months, excelling and impressing all of his peers and superiors. Jackson and Stacey had agreed to a year-long engagement to give themselves time to really save up some money and plan the wedding day of their dreams. They were getting to the home-stretch with three months to go before Stacey became Mrs. Jackson Lucas Howard.

But, lately Jackson had been feeling like something was off...something Stacey wasn't saying. He couldn't figure it out and every time he'd ask her, she would just say everything was fine and nothing was wrong. But, his gut was telling him other-wise. Jackson wasn't one for snooping through phones and emails or anything like that. If it was meant for him to know, it'll be revealed in due time.

And that time came...right around Jackson's twenty-sixth birthday. He was at the firehouse in the kitchen area when one of his colleagues named Aaron walked in talking on his cell phone on speaker. Jackson had his back turned, pouring himself a cup of coffee. He wasn't really paying much attention until he noticed that the voice on the other end of the phone sounded oddly familiar.

"Baby, I miss you! What time are you getting off?" the female voice asked.

"I miss you too, Boo. I should be free in about another hour or two. Question is, are YOU gonna be free?" Aaron asked with emphasis.

"Whatchu mean?! Of course I'll be free for you!"

"Nah, nah! You made it seem like you were busy this weekend or somethin'."

"I mean it's just his birthday or whatever. I'll make up a good *excuse and just promise him plans for tomorrow. Hell, his actual birthday ain't til Monday, anyway. I got time."*

Just then Jackson turned around to face Aaron. He had a stone cold look in his eyes, yet showed no other emotion. He took a long sip of his coffee, never breaking eye contact with Aaron, who was now as white as a ghost. Aaron thought Jackson had left for the day, but didn't know he had offered to cover for one of the other guys who needed to take an extended lunch break. Aaron blinked rapidly and stammered trying to find something to say, but his words failed him.

"Don't worry, Bruh. She'll be free the WHOLE weekend. Trust me," Jackson said matter-of-factly and calmly walked out of the kitchen.
"Hello?!" the female voice shouted through the phone.
"Uh...Baby?" Aaron whispered nervously.
"What? What's wrong witchu?" she asked in frustration.
"He knows."

Silence...

"Oh my God!" Noelle exclaimed. "Are you serious?!"
"Yup," Jackson said simply.
"So, what happened? What did you do?" she asked.
"Once my shift ended, I went home and just kinda let it all sink in. She wasn't home yet. Or maybe she *was* there and left before I got home. I'm not sure."

Jackson went on to say how he flew into a silent, blind rage once the reality of everything set in, and he got extremely pissed! He went through closets, snatching every piece of Stacey's clothing off the hangers and tossing them into a pile on the floor. He then dumped the contents of every drawer full of her stuff onto that same pile. Shampoos, blow dryers, curling irons, jewelry, shoes, photos, even her framed degree hanging on the wall were all snatched up and carelessly chucked onto the pile in the center of the bedroom floor.

There were even sheet sets and other home décor he knew Stacey had brought when she moved in with him. That had to go, too! Jackson aimed to erase any and every part of her existence out of his home and his life.

"She walked in just as I was dismantling her vanity table," Jackson continued. "I could see the crocodile tears forming and her looking for some bullshit story to tell me. I told her to keep it, 'cuz I didn't wanna hear it. I wanted nothing from her, except for her to get her shit outta my floor 'cuz I was tired of stepping over it."

"Baby, you didn't?!" Noelle asked, trying not to smile.

"I sure did. I didn't want an explanation or an apology or an excuse. I didn't even want the damn ring back. Just...go."

Jackson had found a box of black trash bags for Stacey to gather all her things, because he refused to let her pack up the $500 Coach luggage set he had bought her one Christmas. In the middle of Stacey crying and shouting, trying to plead her case, Jackson's phone rang. It was one of his cousins asking what Jackson was up to that night for his birthday weekend. When he said he had no plans, they invited him to come out with them. Jackson quickly changed his clothes, sprayed on some Dolce & Gabbana cologne and grabbed his hairbrush.

"I want you and all this shit outta my house by the time I get back or we're gonna have a real problem. And you know I'm not one to stay out late. So, the clock is ticking," Jackson said flatly while lightly brushing his waves.

Then he simply turned and walked out the front door.

Jackson said that while he was out with his cousins he ran into Aundre. They had actually gone to high school together and were pretty close before graduating and going their separate ways. Aundre was in town visiting family for a few days, but he had been living in Houston for about a year and had recently started working as an EMT with the fire department. When he found out Jackson was a certified firefighter, too, Aundre encouraged him to think about relocating because there were a lot more opportunities available for young firemen in Houston than Memphis. Jackson told him thanks for the advice and that he'd think about it.

"Three months later, I sold my house, packed up my life and here I am," Jackson said, raising his glass of orange juice in salute.

"Wow!" Noelle exclaimed. "Well, first of all, I'm proud of you for just jumping out there and taking the risk to change your whole life,"

"Thank you, Baby," he said with a smile.

"So...have you seen her since then?" she asked, referring to Stacey.

"Once," he said. "I went home for a funeral and she was there. We didn't speak. Well, *I* didn't."

"Why not?"

"Because I didn't need to. I had nothing to say and nothing to gain by forcing myself to engage in pointless conversation. We broke up because she cheated. There's nothing to talk about."

"Makes sense, I guess."

"Wanna hear something funny?"

"Sure."

"The day I left Memphis was supposed to be our wedding date."

Jackson threw up his two fingers in the peace sign and he and Noelle laughed heartily. He shared his story with her to let her know she wasn't a lone target. Cheating, betrayal, and heartbreak is all fair game to any and everyone. It can't always be avoided, but it can absolutely be overcome.

They both chose to leave their pain behind in the place where it happened and go rebuild their lives somewhere else where they could fully focus on their healing.

"I'm proud of you too, Baby," Jackson said sweetly. "You literally came home, back to where your entire life's story started, and you chose to start over. To rewrite from the beginning. You're braver and stronger than you know. And I am so proud of you and who you are. You will get through this, and you're gonna kill it. I'm just grateful I get to witness the phoenix rise."

Jackson grabbed Noelle's hand and brought it to his lips, kissing her knuckles tenderly. The woman sitting across from him was beautiful, smart, successful, resilient and the embodiment of true feminine power. He hated how much her ex and her family had hurt her, because he knew how much she did not deserve any part of it; but he loved that she didn't let it break her. Bent, maybe...but not broken.

Twelve

The morning sunlight threaded through the trees, flickering against the windows of Jackson's pickup truck as he drove down the street. Chaka Khan serenading her "Sweet Thing" floated through the speakers and filled the comfortable silence between Noelle and Jackson as their hands sat suspended in the air with fingers intertwined. He absent-mindedly brought her knuckles up to rest against his lips as he navigated the Tuesday morning traffic.

Their impromptu two-day rendezvous was everything Jackson had hoped it would be. Although the circumstances that brought them together were not the most ideal, he was very pleased with how things took a turn for the better. The images of Noelle's face reflecting ecstasy and pleasure played on a repetitive reel in Jackson's mind, and her sensuous sounds echoed in his ears, drowning out the morning radio show DJs delivering the latest celebrity gossip. A throaty groan escaped out of Jackson at the memory of feeling Noelle's warm mouth wrapped around his manhood last night in the kitchen.

"Penny for your thoughts?" Noelle quipped, interrupting his silent pondering.

"Hmm? Oh, nothing. Just remembered something I need to do," Jackson replied quickly with a smirk.

Jackson turned the corner and continued down Noelle's block, honking the horn at his crew as he rolled by the fire station.

"I really enjoyed our time together these last few days, Jackson," Noelle said sweetly. "Thank you for being there for me and whisking me away from all this craziness going on in my world."

"Thank you for giving me the chance," Jackson said sincerely. "I know with everything you've been through over the years and just this last week, trusting someone else with your feelings and well-being isn't an easy thing to do."

"No, it's not...but you make it easy."

Jackson leaned over and kissed Noelle softly on the forehead, tip of her nose and then her lips, before proceeding through the stop sign at the corner of Noelle's block. Just as they were nearing her house, Jackson noticed a steel gray Dodge Ram pickup truck parked in Noelle's driveway. As he slowly drifted past it to park along the curb, he saw an older gentleman sitting on the top step of the porch.

"Oh, God!" Noelle exclaimed as she palmed her face in frustration
"Baby, who is that?" Jackson asked with a furrowed brow.
"My father," she said flatly with her face still buried in her hand.
"Oh...damn."

Although Jackson looked forward to meeting her father one day, these were not the circumstances he had envisioned for that moment. Dropping off the man's baby girl with an overnight bag in tow, probably didn't set the right tone in Jackson's mind. *This will be interesting*, he thought, before hopping out of the truck and going around to open the passenger side door for Noelle. He grabbed her duffle bag off the backseat, laced his fingers through hers and walked towards the house and Noelle's father, all the while praying his confident poker face would hold up.

Richard Morgan sat comfortably on the concrete steps with his hands resting palms down on his knees. The damp late-November air created light condensation on his glasses, so he removed them and wiped them off with the hem of his red and black checkered button-down shirt. Richard wore his favorite gray cardigan with wooden toggles that he left unfastened. His salt and pepper hair glistened in the morning sunlight that occasionally peeked through the clouds.

Richard placed his freshly cleaned glasses back on his face and watched his beloved daughter walk towards him, escorted by a uniformed gentleman that sparked his curiosity.

"Daddy, what are you doing here?" Noelle asked Richard, sounding slightly annoyed.

"Oh, nothin'. Just catchin' some fresh air and gettin' rained on," Richard replied sarcastically, referring to the light drizzle that had started when Jackson and Noelle pulled up.

"Very funny, Daddy, but I'm still waiting on an answer," Noelle said with a raised eyebrow.

"Ya Mama was drivin' me crazy worryin' 'bout ya not answerin' her calls and carryin' on. So, I'm usin' ya as my excuse to escape her crazy, and to put eyes on ya for myself. Now, hurr'up and open that do'r 'fore my knees and back lock up out here!"

At that moment, Jackson extended his hand to Richard to help him stand up from his seat on the concrete steps of Noelle's front porch. As Richard came to his feet, Jackson took the opportunity to shake his hand for real.

"How you doin', Sir?" Jackson greeted with a smile.

"Just fine, young man. Considerin' my daughter is actin' too damn much like me right now," Richard replied with a smirk as his eyes darted back and forth between his daughter and this friendly stranger.

"Daddy, this is Jackson. Jackson, this is my father, Mr. Richard Morgan, Sr." Noelle introduced the pair dryly.

"Ah, so *you're* Jackson? Heard quite a bit about ya, Son," Richard said as their hand shake ended and he dug his hands into the pockets of his taupe-colored slacks.

"You *have*? From *who*?!" Noelle asked incredulously

"Ya gossipin' sister, mostly." he said with a shrug

"Of course," she said, rolling her eyes.

Jackson excused himself because he had to get to work. He told Richard how glad he was to finally meet him and that he looked forward to seeing him again soon. Noelle walked Jackson back to his truck, their fingers laced together tenderly with him giving her hand a light squeeze of reassurance that everything would be fine. Standing at the open door saying their goodbyes, Jackson gave Noelle a pleading look that said "Please don't make me kiss you in front of your father!" She just giggled, shook her head and kissed the back of Jackson's hand softly before he climbed into his truck, grateful that she understood his nervous plight.

The sound of Jackson's engine revving as he accelerated down the street was confirmation to Noelle that she was now left alone with her father, who she had been avoiding along with everyone else for days. She silently walked past him and headed up the porch steps to her front door. Richard followed closely behind as they entered her home. He removed his shoes and placed them neatly by the front door, then made his way towards the kitchen to take a seat at the round, Maplewood table. Noelle went upstairs to deposit her overnight bag into her bedroom.

Feeling like she needed to buy herself more time to avoid her father's eyes and get her mind together, Noelle began unpacking her bag – removing the dirty clothes and placing them in the hamper, emptying her toiletry bag and putting all the items back in their rightful places in the bathroom. Noelle slid the now empty duffle bag back on the top shelf in her closet, and released a heavy sigh as she closed the closet's accordion doors. Then begrudgingly, she walked out of her bedroom and back downstairs.

She found her father seated at her kitchen table, quietly and calmly flipping through the *Essence* magazine sitting there. Noelle had a feeling this wasn't going to be an easy interaction to avoid, but she was definitely going to try.

"Well, uh…," Noelle started.

"You got coffee?" Richard interrupted without looking up from the article he was reading.

"Wh…uh, yeah I got coffee," she stammered.

"Get an old man a cup, will ya?" he said with a smile while peering over the rims of his glasses.

Noelle looked at the top of Richard's head, as his eyes were now back on the page in front of him. The look she had was one of both confusion and offense, because how dare he just assume she wanted him there long enough to even finish a cup of damn coffee?! But, that's her Daddy. So, with a frustrated huff, Noelle marched over to the coffeemaker and prepped the machine to meet her father's request.

From angrily shoving the teaspoon into the porcelain sugar bowl and dropping three scoops into the black mug she had pulled out for her father, to snatching the refrigerator door open to pull out the coffee cream and slamming the bottle down on the counter. Every motion Noelle made was accompanied by an aggravated huff – all of which Richard was completely unmoved by. He kept right on flipping through the pages of the magazine and waited for Noelle to serve him coffee, despite being an uninvited guest.

Noelle sat the piping hot mug down right on top of the open magazine, drawing her father's eyes up to meet her own. The look she gave him reminded him so much of his wife, Annabelle, that he couldn't help but chuckle.

"What's so funny?" Noelle asked dryly as she stepped away to make a cup for herself.

"You're so much like Anna, it's scary," Richard said, still smiling as he sipped.

"Oh yeah? How so?"

"Them cuttin' eyes."

Noelle smiled against the rim of her mug, because she knew exactly what he meant. She'd seen her mother give that same look to quite a few people before, including Richard when he had finally plucked her last nerve. Funny how he was so good at doing that with all the Morgan women.

"Daddy, you know I love seeing you and all, but what are you doing here?" Noelle mustered up with a heavy sigh.

"I came to check on ya," Richard said plainly.

"Okay, and now that you have?" she said with a shrug and furrowed brow.

"Now that I have...I wanna apologize to you."

"Apologize? For what?"

Richard pushed his mug away as he took a deep breath. There was a pregnant pause between them, less the soft sound of Richard's fingers anxiously drumming against the tabletop. He brought his gaze up to meet Noelle's, and she swore she saw tears brimming in his eyes. She couldn't recall a time where she had ever seen her father be emotional before, and to see it now had her both shocked and intrigued.

"What are you sorry for, Daddy?" Noelle pressed.

Considering all that had happened and the secrets revealed during

Thanksgiving dinner with her family, she wasn't sure she could take another blindsiding confession.

"I'm ya father, Nola," Richard began. "It's my job to protect you from gettin' hurt, in any way, and I failed you. I put ya in the hands of a man who betrayed you. And then finding out ya own kinfolk knew and ain't say nothin', and meanwhile I live with and look at these people day in and day out and never paid attention to what was going on. I'm supposed to keep ya safe...and I..."

Richard exhaled a shaky breath, fighting the tears that threatened to flee his eyes. Noelle reached across the table, taking a hold of her father's hands as her own tears started to form.

"Daddy, you didn't fail me," Noelle reassured him. "You are not responsible for what other people choose to do."

"Yeah, I know that, but..." Richard started, but his words fell short.

"There are alot of people in my life who did fail to take care of me as they should've, but I promise you are not one of them." Noelle said, giving his hand a reaffirming squeeze.

Noelle moved to the chair next to Richard and cupped his face in her hands, swiping away his tears with the pad of her thumb.

"Do you remember when I first moved back home?" Noelle asked softly. Richard nodded.

"You welcomed me home with open arms and no questions or judgements. You never made me feel bad about my marriage falling apart. You gave me exactly what I needed when I needed it, and I couldn't be any more grateful. You were the first man in my life that made me feel the most protected, especially when I was at my weakest. You have never failed me."

Noelle pulled her father into a warm embrace and kissed the top of his head. For a long while, they just held each other, letting their emotions flow with the silence between them echoing what they truly felt in that moment.

The scent of lemongrass and olive oil filled the air in Noelle's kitchen as she prepared dinner for Richard and herself. Chicken farfalle with sundried tomatoes and sprinkled parmesan. Richard had extended his visit with Noelle from a quick drop-in to a nearly all-day thing, and she had to admit she was happy he did. Even though it had only been a few days, Noelle missed her family a lot, especially with her being such a Daddy's Girl. She wasn't ready for a full-fledged family reunion just yet, but this one-on-one time with her father was just what she needed and it was right on time.

"Daddy! Dinner's ready," Noelle called out to the living room.

Richard shuffled his way to the kitchen and Noelle placed two red ceramic dinner plates down on the table, next to two frosted drinking glasses. A pitcher of citrus-peach sweet iced tea sat in the middle of the table. Richard couldn't help but smile at his "Baby Girl," as he called her. Taking care of others and creating a comfortable and inviting space for people to feel welcomed and right at home was something that came so naturally to Noelle. Another trait she had inherited from her mother, and something else that drove Richard crazy about his wife.

"Smells delicious, Baby Girl," Richard praised as he placed a linen napkin in his lap.

"Thank you, Daddy. I hope you like it," Noelle beamed.

"I'm sure I will. You Anna's girl, through and through," he said proudly referring to his wife.

"Yeah, I am!" she quipped with a big smile.

The clinking of forks against plates and murmurs of satisfaction mixed in with the melodic tunes of Charlie Parker, Richard's favorite Jazz musician, filled the air in Noelle's kitchen. After they finished dinner, Noelle brewed some vanilla-chai tea and sliced up some cinnamon crunch pound cake for them to enjoy on the sofa. Richard slowly slurped the hot tea, pondering his next words carefully.

"So," Richard started. "Tell me 'bout ya Mr. Someone from earlier."

"Been wondering how long it was gonna take you to ask," Noelle said with a smile.

"Well, ya know, gotta ease into it," he chuckled.

"I see. Well, his name is Jackson, as you know. He actually works at the fire station down the street, if you can imagine that," Noelle said.

"No kiddin'?!" Richard quipped in surprise.

"Yup, just a few blocks away."

"Well, I'll be! Hmm, so how does he treat ya?"

Noelle paused at the thought of how Jackson treated her and couldn't help but smile. Memories of the past few weeks, and especially the past few days, flooded her mind and sent butterflies fluttering in her stomach. Noelle began telling her father about how amazing things had been between them from the moment they first met up to this past weekend where he literally swooped in like some fictional superhero to save her from the recent emotional drama that threatened her peace of mind. But, nothing was fictional about Jackson Lucas Howard. He was as real as the mug in Noelle's hands...and just as steaming hot.

Jackson made Noelle feel both sensual and secure; passionate and protected; whole and heard. He reminded her of her value and what she meant to him every chance he got, and each time he did, it made her feelings for him grow stronger. The way he listened to her, held her hand, rubbed her feet, kissed her forehead or just simply looked at her in silent, appreciative awe never wavered.

Even the way Jackson introduced himself to Noelle's body each time they were intimate, as if it was the first time every time. This man was everything Eric never was, and Noelle didn't realize how much she had longed for a man like this or that she even wanted a man like this...until Jackson showed up.

"Sounds like ya happy," Richard observed.

"I am, Daddy. I really am," Noelle said cheerfully.

"You scared ain't ya?" he asked, looking at Noelle over the rim of his glasses.

"Shitless," she replied wide-eyed.

Richard exhaled a laugh at Noelle confirming what he already knew. Her history with relationships would make anyone cautious or afraid to take that leap again. So, he definitely understood how she felt, but as her father, Richard knew he couldn't let Noelle remain fearful of going for whatever it was she wanted in life. Even love.

"Well, I know ya grown, but let me just say this," Richard started. "It's okay to be protective of ya'self and ya heart, but don't let ya past get in the way of ya future. Don't let what happened with you and Eric be the only life experience ya cling to. The more you live, you'll find out that love has a funny way of redeemin' itself."

Richard smiled and winked at his beloved daughter as they sealed their moment with a celebratory clink of their tea mugs.

Thirteen

"Welcome to Noelle's. How can we h…"

Debra was adding a client's appointment to the Microsoft Outlook calendar when she heard the windchimes off the salon's front door, signaling someone's arrival. As she looked up to greet them, her voice trailed off when she saw who had just entered.

"Well, well, well," Debra sang as a smile spread across her face at the sight of Jackson standing at the counter.

"How you doin', Ms. Debra?" Jackson greeted her with a smile of his own, his thick Memphis accent covering every word like honey.

"I'm doin' just fine, Sir. How are you?"

"I'm great, actually. Can't complain."

"Wouldn't do any good, right?"

"Exactly."

Debra and Jackson shared a laugh as he asked if Noelle was available. Debra said she was in the back doing inventory and pointed him in that direction. He walked towards the back of the salon, waving and smiling politely at the shop's patrons and staff as he went. He turned down a short hallway to his left and found Noelle standing on a ladder inside the supply closet.

"Hey, Gorgeous," Jackson said sweetly after lightly knocking on the door so as not to scare her.

"Heeyy, you!" Noelle greeted with a wide smile. "What are you doing here?"

"Came to see you," he said as he stepped towards her.

Noelle leaned down from the ladder to give Jackson a kiss. She cupped his face in her hands as he grabbed her waist. They each moaned in satisfaction and exhaled in bliss as their lips connected.

"I missed you," Jackson whispered against Noelle's lips, then kissed her again.

"I missed you too, Lovey." Noelle replied with a smile.

"Mmm, that makes me happy," he said, smiling back.

Noelle kissed Jackson's forehead before turning back to her task at hand.

"What are you doing in here?" Jackson asked while tipping boxes on the shelves to inspect their contents.

"Doing inventory so I can submit my supply order today," Noelle replied as she studied the checklist affixed to the clipboard in her hands.

"Gotcha."

"Baby, can you hand me that box on the floor please?"

Noelle shifted two small boxes around on the shelves to make room for the medium-sized one on the floor. She turned on the ladder to face Jackson, expecting to grab the box from him but was met with his stern expression.

"What?" Noelle asked in a high-pitched voice with a furrowed brow.

"*No*, I cannot hand you that box," Jackson said flatly. "You can tell me where it goes and I'll put it there."

"Oh, good Lord!" Noelle exclaimed with a laugh. "Just put it right here, Mr. Chivalry!"

Jackson put the box full of shampoo bottles on the shelf space Noelle had created and gave her a little smack on the butt, making her giggle as she playfully wiggled her hips. Once she finalized her checklist for the supply order, Jackson finally revealed why he had stopped by the salon on his way to run last minute errands before work.

"So, I got a call from my mom today," he began. "She announced that she and my granny are coming here to spend Christmas with me."
"Oh, my God! Baby, that's so great!" Noelle beamed.

She knew how close Jackson was to his mother and grandmother, especially with being an only child and raised by them both. Living so far away and not being able to travel back home as much, sometimes made holidays hard on him. So naturally, he was ecstatic that they were coming this year.

"Yeah, it is," Jackson said with a smile. "And I'd love for you to spend Christmas with us, too."

His words caught Noelle completely off-guard. She hadn't given much thought to them spending the holiday together. Partly because their relationship was still so new and she was trying to keep her expectations to a minimum. The other part was that she was still on the outs with her own family and any thoughts of Christmas just made her feel extremely agitated and depressed all over again. So, Noelle opted to ignore the holiday season altogether, but now Jackson had shaken her a little with his question.

"Y-you want me to spend Christmas wi-with you a-and your family?" Noelle stammered.

"All I want for Christmas is you, Babe," Jackson replied with a wide grin and a wink.

Noelle laughed shyly and dropped her gaze to the floor, suddenly feeling like a bashful little school girl in front of him. Jackson admitted how happy he was with Noelle and that he could not wait for all his favorite ladies to finally meet each other.

Still standing on the middle step of the ladder, she beckoned Jackson with her finger. He came to stand in front of her, bringing them eye-to-eye probably for the first time ever. Noelle circled her arms around his neck and leaned forward, kissing him softly on the lips. Jackson wrapped his arms around her waist with his strong hands resting right on top of her round butt.

As their lips touched, Jackson tightened his fingers' grip on her flesh, a move that turned Noelle on very much. Their kiss deepened as they held each other tighter, getting lost in their connection. Jackson slowly pulled away from the magically magnetic force of Noelle's lips and rested his forehead against hers.

"So, is that a yes?" Jackson asked in a husky tone.
"That's definitely a yes," Noelle said with a smile.

◇◇◇◇◇◇

"Girl, what did you wear the first time you met Ced's mama?" Noelle asked frantically.

She was on FaceTime with Debra while feverishly rifling through her wardrobe trying to find something "First Meeting" appropriate for Christmas with Jackson's mother and grandmother this weekend.

"Well, technically the first time I actually met her was at a high school football game wearing my dance uniform. So, I don't think I'm the best person to ask," Debra replied laughing.

"Ugh! You are no help!" Noelle shouted before bursting into laughter herself.

It was moments like this when she missed talking to her sister, Shandra, but Noelle still wasn't in a place to be bothered with any of her family just yet. Not even her baby sister. So, she was leaning on Debra's expertise since she had been with the same man for nearly twenty years, and had survived her fair share of family dinners with his mom.

Noelle's own lack of experience was very clear because the only man who ever took her home to meet his mother was her ex-husband, Eric. Mama Rosie, as she was affectionately called, loved Noelle from day one and made sure she never felt nervous or out of place around Eric's family. Honestly, she'd never felt that way around anyone, but something about meeting Jackson's family had her all out of sorts.

"Girl, just wear something cute and festive and let that be it. They're gonna love you no matter what, anyway," Debra said sweetly.

"Thank you, Girl. I really hope so," Noelle said, biting her bottom lip nervously.

Noelle and Debra chatted for a while longer while she finished packing her overnight bag – the same bag that had practically taken up permanent residence on Jackson's bedroom floor for as often as she stayed the night with him.

After ending her call with Debra, making one final check of her packed bag and putting the finishing touches on wrapping Jackson's gifts, Noelle sat everything by her front door to load into her car in the morning. Tomorrow was December 23rd and she had a few clients she let squeeze into her schedule, and then she would be heading to Jackson's.

Since he had to work Christmas night, they planned to do dinner on Christmas Eve and breakfast on Christmas morning. Just thinking about that itinerary made Noelle nervous all over again. With a huff, she turned off the lamp in the living room and stomped in frustration up the stairs to take a bath. Hopefully, that would help her relax.

Noelle placed the cookie sheet with six foil-wrapped sweet potatoes in the oven to bake and stirred the pot of collard and turnip greens cooking on top of the stove. She had come by Jackson's house last night after work to help him prepare for his mom's and grandmother's arrival. Today was Christmas Eve and she and Jackson were in their respective areas getting dinner plans underway. Noelle was manning the kitchen and Jackson was outside on the patio prepping the grill. Their guests were flying in today and would be arriving just in time for the holiday feast.

Noelle was seasoning the chicken quarters, turkey drums and wings, and ribs for Jackson to put on the grill. She was also watching the time tick by faster than she'd like. The closer it got to their arrival time, the more anxious she became, and that was not lost on Jackson at all.

"Where's the fire at, Babe?" Jackson asked jokingly from the doorway of the kitchen.

"What?" Noelle asked in confusion.

"Why are you moving so fast?"

"Oh, was I? I didn't realize it."

"Now you're moving fast *and* talking fast. You okay?"

"Yeah, I'm fine. All good."

Jackson was right. Noelle's words were coming out so fast she was practically speaking in tongues. She had four food projects going on at once, bouncing from the stove to the counter to the island back to the stove and so on. Cabinet doors and drawers were open throughout the kitchen, as well. Jackson could tell she was moving with a lot of frantic and nervous energy, and that her mind was going at a rapid pace from the undue pressure she was placing on herself. He walked up behind her as she stood at the stove, now dropping the macaroni noodles into boiling water.

"Baby, Baby, come here," Jackson said calmly as he grabbed her waist and pulled her towards him.

"Wha-What?!" Noelle asked in agitation, still holding the half-empty box of macaroni.

"I need you to do something for me," he said.

"I'm already doing one hundred other things, but sure. What *else* do you need, Jackson?"

"I need you to breathe and calm down. I'm right here with you and I got your back. You're good. Everything's good. Breathe, Baby."

Noelle exhaled a heavy sigh as her eyes fluttered closed. She took several deep breaths at Jackson's coaching and could feel her nerves settling down. She nodded with each exhale as he soothingly rubbed her arms and kissed the top off her head – reassuring her that everything will be fine and there was nothing to worry about.

After Jackson made sure Noelle was okay, he headed to the airport to pick up his visitors. Noelle took full advantage of that momentary reprieve to do just as Jackson commanded – breathe. She turned all the pots on the stove down to a low simmer, checked on the sweet potatoes baking in the oven and peeked at the grill outside to make sure Jackson hadn't left an open flame going. When all fire safety concerns were addressed, Noelle darted upstairs to take a much needed, relaxing shower.

◇ ◇ ◇ ◇ ◇ ◇

Jackson entered the house, followed by his mother, Dana and his grandmother, Ester. They were immediately greeted by the joyful sounds of Luther Vandross singing about "Mistletoe Jams" and the delectable scents of Soul Food Magic coming from the kitchen.

Dana and Ester stepped across the threshold into the foyer shivering and fussing, glad to finally be out of the cold. Between their crowded, uncomfortably cold flight to the equally crowded and cold airport and every other chaotic traveling event one could imagine, they had never been more grateful to be in the house.

"Babe?!" Jackson called out to Noelle as he hung up his mother's coat in the hall closet next to the stairs.
"You rang?" Noelle replied gleefully, emerging from the kitchen carrying a serving tray.

On the tray were four glass stout mugs with a cinnamon stick inside of each one. Two were filled with a homemade spiced rum gingerbread eggnog cocktail and the other two had caramel apple bourbon hot cider. She also had a small plate of glazed cocktail wieners with toothpicks and napkins.

"Merry Christmas, everybody! Let these warm you up," Noelle sang, still smiling as she held the tray out for each of them to choose a drink.

Everyone made their selections and thanked her profusely. The sounds of happy moans and murmurs told Noelle they were pleased with her holiday concoctions, which was lucky for her because it was the first time she'd made them.

"Mmm, Baby this is really good," Jackson said before taking another generous sip and planting a kiss on her cheek.

"Yes, this is delicious! I hope there's more," his mother, Dana, exclaimed.

"If it is, I'm drinking it up! So, you better enjoy that *one* while you can!" his grandmother, Ester said pointedly and did a little shoulder shimmy and two-step.

"I'm glad you like it," Noelle said with a laugh.

"I love it! First time meeting and you serve me homemade eggnog with the liquor in it?! I knew I'd like you!" Dana said, raising her glass in appreciation before taking another hefty sip.

Trying to suppress his own laugh, Jackson took a moment to make proper introductions.

"Ma, Nani, this is my baby, Noelle," he said proudly. "Noelle, this is my mom, Dana Elise, and my Nani, Ester Louise. Everything that makes me who I am, is their fault."

The three women exploded into a fit of giggles and Dana swiped at her son's arm for the joke he made. Jackson showed his guests to their room and dropped off their luggage in the corner of the bedroom. There were two twin beds neatly made up with foil-wrapped *Hershey's* kisses sprinkled on the pillows of each bed. Noelle had come in earlier and straightened up the room, made the beds and left the sweet treats for Jackson's mom and grandmother while he was on the patio cleaning and prepping the grill. The soft, homey touches she made did not go unnoticed by Jackson, and he made a mental note to *thank* her later.

Jackson soon got to work placing the chicken quarters and ribs on the dual racks of the grill and brushed on his homemade marinade. He heard the sliding patio door open and saw his mother, Dana step through it. He smiled at the sight of her and she smiled back.

"Hey, Ma. What's up?" Jackson greeted his mother.

"Hey, Baby. Just coming out here to check on you," Dana replied, taking another sip from the mug in her hand.

"Uh, how many of those have you had, Ma'am?" he asked with a raised eyebrow.

"This is just my first one," she answered in a high pitched tone.

"Ma, that can't be the same eggnog Noelle gave you when you first got here?"

"Oh, no. *This* is spiked peppermint hot cocoa."

Jackson smacked his lips and shook his head before reaching for the mug, asking to get a "lil' sip." Dana handed him the drink and laughed at his shocked expression after tasting the hot cocoa and realizing how good it was.

"That woman of yours is dangerous in the kitchen *and* behind the bar!" Dana exclaimed with a chuckle after he handed her the drink back.

"That she is," Jackson said blissfully, as he looked through the kitchen window to steal a glance at Noelle, who was laughing with his grandmother at the island.

"Hmmm," Dana mused as she took another sip of hot cocoa and pulled the lapels of her jacket closer together.

"What happened?" he asked with a raised brow.

"You love her, don't you?"she asked, trying to hide her smile.

Jackson paused at his mother's question, as her words were his inner-most thoughts brought to life. He had been contemplating his feelings for Noelle for quite some time and wanted to be very clear and certain about them. Because of both their histories with love, the last thing he wanted to do was jump to conclusions about how he may or may not feel about Noelle, especially when he wasn't sure if those feelings were mutual. However, Jackson was never one to lie to himself, and he certainly could never lie to his mama, so he wasn't going to start now.

"Yes, Ma'am, I do," Jackson said firmly, looking Dana directly in the eyes.

A huge smile spread across Dana's face at her son's confession and her eyes nearly filled with tears. Knowing what Jackson had been through in his last relationship with Stacey, she often wondered, and worried, if he would ever give love another chance. She was so pleased to hear that he had.

"Oh, Baby, I'm so happy for you!" Dana exclaimed as she hugged him tightly around the waist.

"Thanks, Ma," Jackson replied with a chuckle, hugging his mother back.

"No, I'm serious! I'm so glad you found somebody who makes you happy and helped you believe in love again. You deserve to have every bit of the love you give away to everybody else returned back to you a hundred times over. I really think you've found that with Noelle."

"You really think so?"

"I really, really do."

Dana and Jackson hung out by the grill for a little while longer, letting the marinade cook into the meat a little more, before heading inside to join Noelle and Nani Ester in the kitchen. Christmas Eve dinner went on without a hitch. Dana and Nani Ester raved about Noelle's cooking and hostess skills, and complimented her on hiding her nervousness very well. Noelle laughed at the mention of it because as hard as she tried to hide it, it was still noticeable to everyone, but she appreciated the compliment, nonetheless.

After dinner was over, Jackson, Dana & Nani Ester went into the living room to enjoy some sweet potato pie by the fireplace. He asked Noelle if she wanted any help cleaning up the kitchen, but she assured him that she would much rather he go spend as much time with his family as he could, especially since he had to work tomorrow. Noelle could hear the echoes of laughter and joyous conversation coming from the living room while she loaded the dishwasher.

The sounds brought a smile to her face and a slight twinge of pain to her heart, because she truly missed that kind of camaraderie with her own family. She had actually received several texts and voicemails from her parents, siblings and extended family saying how much they missed her, and inviting her to Christmas dinner. Noelle was torn between standing firm in her grudge and anger towards everyone, or giving in to her longing to be back in the fold of the Morgan-Douglas clan and all its crazy.

It seems like the universe knew exactly what Noelle needed in that moment, because in walked Nani Ester with her empty mug and plate. Noelle asked if she wanted anything else to eat or drink because the kitchen was still open.

"No, thank you, Baby. If I eat anythin' else, imma bust!" Nani Ester said, rubbing her full belly.

"Alright, now. If you change your mind, just let me know," Noelle said sweetly.

"I will. So, you goin' to see ya folks tomorrow since Jackey's gonna be workin'?"

"Uh, no Ma'am, I'm not."

"Why? Holidays are the time to be with ya loved ones."

"Uh...Umm...It's a bit of a long story that I'd rather not get into right now."

"I see. Well, I'm always one to mind my own bid'ness, so I'll just say this. Don't let the sin of one be the fault of all."

"What do you mean, Nani?"

"Meaning whatever happened wasn't *everybody's* fault. Don't punish them or ya'self by putting up walls between y'all. Now *whoever* did do *whatever*? You leave them right where they fucked up at. Don't forgive *nothing* you ain't ready to. But, you *should* go be with ones you love and who you know love you. That's just my two cents that you didn't ask for."

And with that, Nani Ester gave Noelle a kiss goodnight on the cheek and shuffled her house-shoe clad feet out of the kitchen and headed upstairs to bed, leaving a stunned Noelle behind to contemplate her words.

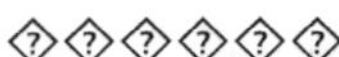

Jackson locked the patio door and closed the blinds after coming back inside from cleaning off the grill. He knew he wouldn't feel like doing it anytime tomorrow before going into work for a fourteen hour shift. So, it was tonight or never. After doing a quick perimeter walk around the first floor of his house to make sure no stray dishes or lit candles were strewn about, he shut off all the lights and headed upstairs.

He could hear the unmistakable sounds of Noelle singing in the shower when he walked into his bedroom. The visual of her nude body covered in suds and water flashed in Jackson's mind and suddenly he, too, needed a shower now. He pushed his bedroom door closed and quickly stripped out of his white t-shirt, blue jeans and gray boxers and strolled towards the bathroom in all his naked glory.

Jackson pushed the bathroom door open with his fingertips, peeking around it to see Noelle behind the steamed up glass shower doors. The sight of water streaming down her back and over her curves instantly made him hard. He closed the bathroom door and walked up to the shower, tapping lightly on the glass. Noelle jumped at the sound and laughed at herself as she turned her head to look at him. Seeing his perfectly sculpted naked body standing there made her eyes widen and mouth water.

"Want some company?" Jackson asked after sliding the shower door open.

"Always," Noelle replied, a flirty smile forming on her face.

Jackson stepped into the shower, closing the door behind him. He reached for Noelle, running his strong hand up her back until it came to rest on the nape of her neck. She threw her head back, giving him full view and access to her throat. Jackson came up behind her until his firm manhood rested between her cheeks. Noelle released a passionate sigh when she felt his body pressed against hers. He began to massage her neck and shoulders as he kissed along her pulse.

"I want to thank you," Jackson whispered in a husky tone against her ear.

"For what?" Noelle exhaled in a whisper of her own.

"For being amazing, and I don't just mean today," he complimented.

"Me? Amazing? Nooo," she replied playfully.

Jackson spun her around to face him, pressing her back against the wall of the shower. He stood so close to her that nothing but water from the shower head was between them. He clasped her face in his palms, tilting her head back so he could fully access her lips. Jackson lowered his mouth to hers, kissing her with every ounce of desire he felt burning inside of him. He slipped his fingers into her hair and gripped it tightly as he continued to devour her mouth, inhaling every whimper and moan she released.

Noelle pressed her fingers into Jackson's lower back, clinging on for dear life as she tried not to melt away down the drain. The feel of his firm fingers on her scalp, hard Adonis frame pressed against her soft breast and abdomen, and his firm manhood rested against her pelvis all sent Noelle's mind into a tailspin. Their heavy breaths mixing with the shower's steam while fiery passion coursed through their veins all rivaled any five alarm fire Jackson had ever faced.

He slid his hands down her body, cuffing her butt and hoisting her up until she wrapped her legs around his waist. Jackson slipped into her body with ease, and the feel of her warm center enveloping him made his knees buckle. He pressed his face into her neck to muffle his moans while she bit down on his shoulder to quiet her own.

Jackson rocked his hips, gliding in and out of Noelle with slippery precision. She wrapped her arms around his neck and gripped the back of his head tightly with her mouth close to his ear so he could hear her cries of pleasure loud and clear. Every moan of his name, every profane word spoken, every rake of her nails across his skin made Jackson lose his mind. He pumped into her faster, no longer wanting to fight back his animalistic need for the woman in his arms.

"Jackson!" Noelle cried in his ear as she tightened her hold around his neck and the walls of her core around his manhood.

"Yeah, Baby? You like that?" Jackson grunted against her face as he ground his hips into hers.

"I love it! Fuck!" she moaned.

"You gonna cum for me?" he coaxed, pumping faster.

"Only if you cum for me," she teased through panting breaths, locking her ankles behind his back.

"Hell yeah, imma cum for you!"

He gripped her hips, fingertips pressed firmly into her flesh and held her close as he thrust harder...deeper...faster. He kissed her lips hard, trying to suppress both their moans getting louder and echoing off the shower walls any more than they already were. Noelle screamed into Jackson's mouth through their joined lips as an orgasm crashed through her body, making her cling even tighter to his shoulders. Jackson groaned loudly when he felt her walls tighten around him – sending him right over the edge, following Noelle as they both fell into an oblivion of ecstasy.

Finally catching their breaths and getting their bearings, Jackson lowered Noelle back down until her feet met the shower floor. They fell into a fit of hazy giggles, still feeling high on cloud nine. The water was growing tepid, so they showered quickly before it became too cold. Jackson swaddled Noelle in a large bath sheet, then scooped her up in his arms, carrying her across the threshold back into his bedroom. He playfully flipped her out of his arms onto the bed before climbing in next to her. They laughed heartily as Noelle fussed about him getting the sheets wet because neither of them had fully dried off.

"They're about to get wetter," Jackson said in a deep, sensuous tone as he snatched the towel off her body, dropping it into a terry cloth puddle on the floor beside the bed.

Noelle pulled into the familiar driveway, staring at the red front door adorned with a beautiful handmade wreath. Just like every other Christmas over the last four years, she stopped by Mama Rosie's house to drop off her gifts and specially requested spiced rum cake with cinnamon buttercream frosting; but year five was a little different. This year, Noelle had no idea what she would possibly be walking into when she rang that woman's doorbell, now that Eric was back in town parading around his new fiancée, who just so happened to be her cousin.

Noelle had been doing a banner job of avoiding them over the last month or so, but all that hard work could come crashing down with one little knock on that red door. Releasing a nervous, exasperated sigh, Noelle grabbed the gift bag and cake off the passenger seat and got out of her car. Before she could even make it up to the porch, the front door flew open and a short, petite light-skinned woman stepped outside.

Rose Janette Pastor, or Mama Rosie, was a small framed woman with short sandy brown hair that still had yet to show signs of graying, even at nearly seventy-years of age. Her face was peppered with light brown freckles and she always looked like she glowed from the inside out, and today was no different.

Mama Rosie beamed with joy at the sight of Noelle outside her door and quickly rushed to hug her, paying no mind to the brisk chill in the air of a hazy Christmas morning. Noelle's smile was just as wide and eyes just as bright when she wrapped her free arm around her former mother-in-law and wished her a Merry Christmas.

"Thank you, Baby! Merry Merry to you too!" Mama Rosie greeted, giving her guest another tight squeeze. "Come on in."

Noelle stepped across the threshold into the single-story ranch home where Eric had grown up, took his first steps, said his first words and proposed to Noelle – all in this same living room that looked fresh out of an episode of *Dynasty* with plastic draped over everything. She followed Mama Rosie further into the home until they ended up in the kitchen, where she was still in the throes of preparing Christmas dinner.

"I see not much has changed," Noelle joked, looking at the plethora of pots and pans being readied for the stove.

"Chil'e, nothin' but the date on the calendar," Mama Rosie replied with a chuckle as she slipped the apron over her head and tied the strings behind her back.

"You hosting again this year?" Noelle asked.

"Yeah, ya know I don't eat at e'rrybody's house," Mama Rosie said, cutting her eyes at Noelle and smirking.

"Oh, I remember," Noelle said with a laugh. "Well, I don't think this is gonna be enough cake for everybody."

"What *everybody*?! That's for me!" Mama Rosie exclaimed, pulling the covered cake plate across the island towards herself.

Noelle laughed loudly at the display. She knew Mama Rosie and Eric had a large family that liked to gather for major holidays, like Christmas;

and she usually handled hosting everybody because she really didn't trust other folks' cleanliness, nor did she feel like driving all over Houston in holiday traffic. When Noelle and Eric were still in college, she had made the rum cake as a contribution to Christmas dinner just because she didn't want to show up empty handed, even though he and his mom assured her it wasn't necessary. However, the minute Mama Rosie tried a slice, she immediately assigned Noelle the duty of making her a cake every Christmas until she said differently. That was nearly ten years ago, and her demands hadn't changed.

Noelle noticed how quiet the house still was at almost noon, and decided to risk asking where Eric and Marguerite were. As soon as she mentioned their names, Mama Rosie looked over the rim of her glasses in near disgust.

"See, now we were havin' such a good time," Mama Rosie said sarcastically, shaking her head.

"Oooh, don't be like that," Noelle said with a giggle, shaking her head in return.

"You right. It's the Lord's birthday. I'll be nice," Mama Rosie replied, plastering a fake smile on her face.

"Mama Rosie!" Noelle exclaimed, palming her face.

Mama Rosie informed Noelle that the twosome had planned to have breakfast with Marguerite's mother, Gladys, that morning and would be by later on for dinner with Eric's side of the family. She made it very clear that she was in no way looking forward to them being in her house parading around like a couple, but again, "it's Jesus's birthday." So, she promised to play nice.

"Well, I'm glad you're choosing peace instead of violence today, Mama Rosie," Noelle complimented, giving a playful golf clap.

"You know how hard that is for me," Mama Rosie said, jokingly placing the back of her hand against her forehead.

"Oh, I know. So, how *are* you feeling about these pending nuptials, if Christmas has you so bothered?" Noelle asked with genuine concern.

"Still crossin' my fingers it don't get that far," Mama Rosie said plainly as she put a pan of dressing in the oven.

Noelle's eyes widened at Mama Rosie's bluntness, especially knowing how serious she was with that statement. Rose Pastor was never one to mince words or spare feelings when it came to speaking honestly. If it was on her mind, it was coming out of her mouth, and if she said it behind your back, it only came after she had already said it to your face.

So, if she was telling Noelle her hopes of the marriage not happening, then it was without any doubt Eric and Marguerite already knew her feelings, as well. Noelle grimaced a little at the thought of how uncomfortable that probably was for them, but then shrugged dismissively because they damn sure didn't care how uncomfortable any of this was for her.

"You know, Eric told me about Thanksgivin'," Mama Rosie said softly, invading Noelle's thoughts.

"He did?" Noelle asked, her voice high and face frowned up.

"He did. And I am so sorry," Mama Rosie said earnestly.

"Aww, you don't have to apologize. You didn't do anything," Noelle replied with a wave of her hand.

"True, but he's my son. Fruit of my loins and labor."

"He also was and still is a grown man responsible for his own decisions."

"Also true, but I know my child. He will find any way to justify his own foolishness and feel like he doesn't have to apologize to anyone for anything. And it's you. My Nola. I can't have that. You're owed an apology, and if nobody else is gonna say it, I will. I'm so sorry, Baby."

Noelle could feel the heat behind her eyes as the tears formed. She felt Mama Rosie's kind words hit the center of her heart and couldn't help but get emotional. This wasn't the first time Eric's mother had taken up the helm to apologize for his misdeeds, but every time she did, Noelle brushed it off. Not because she didn't believe the apology to be genuine, but because Rose Pastor shouldn't have to repent for his grown ass, in Noelle's mind.

Mama Rosie came around the island to hug Noelle, who was losing her fight against the flood of tears threatening to burst through. The sweet matriarch rocked her gently, whispering tender words of motherly wisdom and sincerity. She cupped Noelle's face in her hands, making their eyes meet.

"You listen to me," Mama Rosie prompted. "Eric is my one and only and I love him with everythin' I have in me, because that's how it has to be. That's not the case for you. Don't let him be the only one moving on and finding happily ever afters. He may have broken ya heart once, but he didn't ruin ya life. Live it!"

Noelle silently nodded her head as the tears continued to flow. She wanted so badly to tell Mama Rosie about Jackson and the most un-expected newfound happiness she was experiencing just by being with him, but the lump in her throat wouldn't let any words come out. So, she just absorbed the sage words of encouragement and let it fertilize the garden of love growing inside of her – not just a love for herself, but the love she was beginning to feel for Jackson. Something she had often doubted she'd ever feel again, until that one fateful day when he walked into her shop and her life.

Noelle hugged Mama Rosie, clinging tightly to her warmth and her words. Even though it had been years since she and Eric divorced, there was nothing or no one that could change the way these two women felt about each other or tear them from each other's lives. She was her "Nola." Her "forever daughter-in-law," no matter what, and Noelle would always love Mama Rosie with all her heart.

Mama Rosie gave Noelle another tight squeeze and kiss on the cheek before pulling away to grab some plates and coffee cups out of the cabinet. She sat the dishes on the ceramic countertop with a loud clink.

"Now, let's see what this cake talkin' 'bout before these freeloadin' folks get here," Mama Rosie said with a wink.

"Yes, Ma'am," Noelle chuckled as she popped the top on the cake plate and grabbed a knife from the butcher's block.

Noelle spent another hour with Mama Rosie sharing cake, coffee and gossip before heading back to Jackson's house. She wanted to be sure to see him before he went to work and left her to fend for herself in keeping his mother and grandmother occupied and entertained. After last night's Christmas Eve dinner and cocktails, Noelle certainly felt more at ease around the ladies, but now Jackson wouldn't be there to play buffer.

Oh, well. They were gonna find out about my crazy someday. Might as well be today, she thought to herself as she merged onto the highway heading back to Jackson's house.

Fourteen

"If I drop this damn thing one more time!" Noelle huffed to herself in the bathroom.

Nervously, and probably against her better judgment, she had decided to attend her family's annual New Year's Eve party. It would be the first time she'd be in the same room with any of them since the "Turkey Turn-Up" event formerly known as Thanksgiving. Though she had appreciated Nani Ester's encouraging words, she opted to forego Christmas with her family, simply because she needed just a little more time to get over it all...or at least try to.

Now she was standing in her bathroom, anxiously trying to apply her makeup, but she kept dropping her brushes or eyeliner or the eyeshadow palette...TWICE! She was slowly, but surely, becoming overwhelmed by it all. However, she promised herself and Jackson that she would push through and ring in the new year surrounded by love, no matter what.

After she finally wrangled a solid soft glam with bold red lip look together, Noelle sluggishly headed to her bedroom to get dressed. She opted to wear her hair in its natural state of loose curls that draped across the top of her shoulders. Her outfit consisted of a black midi charmeuse wrap dress with a faux knot at the waist, a high front split and deep v-neckline.

She accessorized with gold bangles adorned with crystals and glitter, a gold Y-necklace with a circle pendant that hung down the middle of her chest and accentuated the v-neckline perfectly. An assortment of rings on each hand, a pair of large gold hoops with crystal trim and black strappy heels that tied up her calves pulled her final look together.

Noelle assessed her reflection in the floor length mirror in her bedroom and decided that even if the entire night goes straight to hell doused in gasoline, at least she looked damn good! She had just flipped her hair over to the right, creating a seductive frontal side-part when she heard the front door open and Jackson calling out to her. Noelle retrieved her black clutch off the bed and headed down the stairs to meet him.

Jackson had let himself in after knocking a few times and getting no answer. He was on pins and needles about tonight. For himself, because this was his first time meeting Noelle's family, and he would be meeting everybody all at once. He also had concerns for her, because even though she said she was fine and in a good place since the Thanksgiving fiasco, in the back of his mind he wasn't sure what to expect. No matter what, though, Jackson would be by her side every step of the way.

He heard Noelle descending the stairs and turned around to greet her, but every possible word in his mind evaporated and was immediately replaced by raw, hot, animalistic lust. His skin felt flushed, his breathing became heavy and his eyes darkened with desire. Jackson took measured, yet hurried, steps toward Noelle just as she made it to the bottom stair.

He firmly grabbed her by the throat and hungrily kissed her mouth. Noelle gasped in shock at first, but as the kiss intensified, she moaned in satisfaction. With his other hand, Jackson sank his fingers into the soft fleshiness of Noelle's butt, pressing her body hard against his. Noelle wrapped her arm around Jackson's neck and massaged the back of his head. Jackson licked and nipped at Noelle's lips as he slowly pulled away from the kiss.

The look in Jackson's eyes screamed in deafening volumes and Noelle understood every unspoken word. So, she happily obliged when Jackson turned her around and bent her forward so her hands were pressed against the middle step while her feet stayed planted on the floor. Jackson lightly pushed the heels of her feet apart, spreading her legs open and pushing the hem of the dress up to her waist. The sight of Noelle's round butt made his mouth water.

"Jackson," Noelle started with a sultry giggle. "Baby, we have to g..."

Her words trailed off and were replaced by a soft gasp and moan as she felt Jackson's warm, wet lips press against the skin of her hip and his thumb gently rubbing at the opening of her core. Jackson hooked the material of her thong around his thumb, pulled it to the side and slid into her hot flesh in one smooth motion. His sharp intake of breath matched hers as he entered her body. He gripped Noelle's hips tightly as he thrust deeper and deeper into her. The feel of Jackson's hard manhood moving in and out of her, made Noelle scream in ecstasy as she dug her nails and heels into the carpeted steps.

Jackson moaned and groaned loudly as he quickened his pace, pushing both of them closer and closer to the edge. Noelle went over first as her body tightened, back arched upward and her knees buckled. Knowing she just came drove Jackson wild and brought him to the brink. He could feel his toes curl inside his dress shoes and he found his release. The sounds of sexual bliss echoed off the walls followed by drunken, euphoric laughter.

Jackson fell forward and rested his head in the middle of Noelle's back, trying to catch his breath. He then pulled her back up to standing as he slowly slid out of her core. Jackson situated her thong back into position and pulled her dress back down, trying his best to recapture the look she worked so hard to put together.

"Hey, Baby," Jackson said hazily as he kissed the side of her neck.

"Hey," Noelle said with a delirious laugh. "Well, that's a helluva start to the night."

"You know how I do."

Noelle climbed the stairs with wobbly legs and headed for the bathroom to fix herself back up after Jackson's ravaging. After a quick makeup retouch, "bird bath," and final check of her outfit, Noelle darted back downstairs to grab her coat, then they headed out the door. During the car ride to the venue, she felt a renewed sense of calm about the night. No matter what happened or who might be there, the tone for her evening was already set, thanks to Jackson, and there was nothing that could or would change that.

Noelle and Jackson arrived at the Hilton Inn & Suites near the Houston Airport where her family had rented out one of the event rooms for their party. Every year for the last ten years, both sides of her family would collaborate on a big New Year's Eve party. It was a great way to not only bring in the new year surrounded by family, but it was also a much cheaper alternative than trying to go out anywhere in Houston on such a night. The festivities called for semi-formal, dressed-to-impress attire and offered a DJ and open bar. All-in-all, a recipe for a good time.

Jackson held Noelle's hand tightly as they walked across the parking lot towards the doors of the hotel. Patrons were milling about in the lobby as they followed the signs to the ballroom where her family would be. When they rounded the corner and were just steps away from the room, Noelle made a beeline for the ladies room. Jackson hung out in the hallway waiting for her to come back. Just as he checked the time on his watch, he heard someone call his name.

Jackson turned to his right and spotted Aundre in the hall and a smile spread across his face. They walked toward each other and slapped hands.

"What's good, Bruh? Whatchu doin' here?" Jackson asked, smirking.

"Same as you probably," Aundre said with a smirk of his own.

"Meeting the family, huh? You ready for this?" Jackson asked.

"Too late to turn back now, ain't it?" Aundre replied with a laugh.

"There you are! I turn around for two seconds and you just disappear!" a woman's voice scolded from behind them.

The two men turned around and were greeted by the stern-faced beauty, Shandra. She was fussing at Aundre and then stopped short when she realized Jackson was standing next to him. Almost immediately, tears formed in her eyes as she broke into a huge smile. Shandra rushed into Jackson's arms and hugged him tightly, because she knew his presence meant her wish had come true...or at least she hoped so.

"Is...is she here?" Shandra asked, her eyes pleading and voice cracking with desperation.

"Yeah, she's in the bathroom," Jackson said softly as he stroked her shoulder comfortingly.

Shandra exhaled a sigh of relief hearing confirmation that she would see her big sister today. Just then, Noelle emerged from the bathroom and Jackson waved her over. Shandra turned to see Noelle walking towards them and immediately ran to her sister. The two crashed into each other, clinging together in a tight embrace.

"You better not be crying!" Noelle said as she held on to her sister.

"Oh, girl, my makeup is done!" Shandra said in between sobs and giggles.

"Dammit, Shandy!" Noelle shouted as she gave over to her own happy tears.

The two sisters pulled apart and wiped each other's tear and mascara stained faces with the pads of their thumbs. Noelle softly kissed Shandra's forehead before lacing their fingers together and dashing back to the bathroom once again, now to check both their makeup.

Jackson and Aundre were still standing in the hallway waiting for their dates to come back when the ladies' father, Richard, came walking by with one of their uncles. He was holding an empty decanter and previously lit cigar. He stopped short when he spotted the two men once he recognized who they were. Richard told his brother-in-law that he'd meet him inside shortly and made his way over to Jackson and Aundre.

"Well, hey there, Boys," Richard's gruff baritone broke through the noise of the hallway.

"Hello, Sir. Good to see you again," Jackson greeted him with a firm handshake.

"How are you, Mr. Morgan? Happy New Year to you," Aundre said, extending his hand next.

"Same to you. What y'all doin' out here? There's a very expensive party goin' on right in there," Richard said pointing towards the large oak double doors of the ballroom.

Jackson explained that they were waiting for their dates to come out of the bathroom and they would be right in. Richard gave a short nod of understanding, then insisted they come inside and join him at the bar for a round of drinks. Feeling uneasy about rejecting Richard's invitation, Jackson and Aundre shared a knowing look before saying, "After you," in unison as they followed him into the party.

The raucous sounds of laughter, chatter and the harmonious stylings of Frankie Beverly and Maze bounced off every wall in the room. Everyone was dressed to the nines in their semi-formal, black tie, sequins and glitter-adorned best, including Mr. Richard Morgan, himself. He wore a charcoal gray tuxedo with a crisp black dress shirt, smokey gray satin cumberbun, tie and pocket square accents. Black velvet Italian loafers pulled the entire look together. Jackson and Aundre took notice of his attire and offered a very well-deserved compliment.

"I see you went all out for tonight, huh? You lookin' pretty snazzy there, Mr. Morgan." Jackson said charmingly.

"Man! I feel underdressed standing next to you," Aundre seconded.

"Thank you, Boys," Richard said graciously. "Yeah, the Missus got it right with this one, but don't tell her I said that."

The three men shared a laugh as they headed towards the bar. Jackson took a look around the banquet room as he trailed behind Richard and Aundre. With this being his first time seeing Noelle's family, he was taken aback by how large it was, especially knowing this wasn't even everybody. Most of the round tables set for ten were full, and others only had two or three empty seats left. The dance floor was packed with revelers glowing under the flickering strobe lights and sweating to the oldies. Waitstaff weaved through the partygoers with trays of drinks and hors d'oeuvres with expert precision. It was all a sight to behold.

Having been raised by his mom and grandmother, he only got to grow up around one side of his family, and while he did have a lot of extended family by way of his mom's siblings, it was nothing like this. *I hope she don't expect me to remember all of these people*, Jackson thought to himself.

"Tommy, get me three Johnny Walker's neat," Richard shouted over the music at the bartender as he slid his emptied glass across the bar top.

Tommy grabbed the glass with his left hand without looking, twirled the bottle of scotch in his right hand, pulled two more glasses from under the bar and filled them all in one fluid motion. He placed one glass on a small white square napkin in front of each of them. They all placed some money in the tip jar as they grabbed their drinks.

Richard motioned for Aundre and Jackson to follow him to the other end of the bar in a quieter corner. As he followed behind Richard, Jackson spotted Noelle and Shandra coming through the double doors into the party. He smiled at the sight of her, amazed at how she glowed so effortlessly and how infectious her laughter was. Even over the loud music and ongoing conversations, he could hear her voice, so warm and sweet like melted caramel. It was a sound he wanted to hear every day for the rest of his life. He was certain of it.

Noelle walked into the party arm-in-arm with Shandra and was immediately bombarded by aunts, uncles, cousins, family friends and the like. Infinite hugs, kisses and "I missed you. It's so good to see you!" greetings. Noelle navigated the crowd gracefully and graciously while trying to keep her emotions in check. She hadn't realized how much she'd missed being around her people until just now. Though it had only been a month, it felt like a lifetime ago since she had last shared laughs and a meal with her nearest and dearest.

Noelle was maintaining a good handle on her nerves right up until she saw her mom, Annabelle. They both lost the battle and the tears flowed as they rushed into each other's arms. Annabelle had never held her daughter tighter than she did at that moment. Noelle wrapped her arms around her mother's waist and lay her head on her chest, never wanting to let go. It was a moment long overdue.

An equally teary eyed Shandra rushed over and hugged them both as Annabelle repeatedly whispered, "Thank you, Jesus!" After a few minutes the three of them released from their embrace and Annabelle, in true motherly fashion, wiped her daughters' tear-stained cheeks and placed kisses there. She then walked them over to the table to say hello to their brother and grandmother.

After smothering her grandmother in "some shuga," Noelle made her rounds trying to speak to as many people as she could, while simultaneously searching the room for Jackson. She hadn't seen him since she and Shandra came out of the bathroom. She figured he couldn't have gone far, but losing sight of him and Aundre made her a little nervous, especially with some of her messy relatives running around.

Just as the thought occurred to her, Noelle heard the familiar cackle of her cousin Marguerite, even over the DJ. Noelle looked around the room until she spotted her, gave a thumbs up after clocking her location and abruptly turned to head in the opposite direction. She did the move so quickly that she nearly crashed into Eric, who grabbed her arm trying to avoid impact.

"Whoa!" Eric exclaimed.

"Sorry," Noelle said dryly after realizing who it was.

"No, that's my bad. Should've announced myself," he offered with a half smile.

"I promise, that will never be necessary," she retorted as she went to step around him.

Eric sidestepped, blocking Noelle's path and making her take a step back. Her eyebrows knitted together in the middle of her forehead and her eyes narrowed in confusion.

"What?" Noelle asked in annoyance.

"Look, I...H-How are you, Nola?" Eric stammered.

"I'm fine," she replied in a flat tone, eyes still narrowed.

"You look *great*," he complimented.

"Eric, what do you want? Small talk really isn't our thing."

"Well, uh, I really just wanted to make sure you're okay. I hadn't seen you since, well you know. And I was worried about you."

Noelle scoffed and frowned at his words. He sounded so ridiculous and practically offensive to her, if she were being honest.

"Oh, so *now* you're worried about how your actions and piss poor ways may affect me?" Noelle asked incredulously.

"I...Noelle, please," Eric huffed.

"Please what? Huh?!" she demanded as she squared her shoulders and tilted her head.

"There you are," a husky baritone drawled from behind Eric.

Noelle immediately felt a thump reverberate within her as her knees weakened and heart skipped a beat just at the sound of his voice. Jackson brushed past Eric and held Noelle's gaze captive with each measured step he took towards her. Once they were face-to-face, Jackson stretched out his hand to pass her a lemon drop martini. Just as Noelle's fingers grazed his while grabbing the glass, Jackson leaned in and kissed her softly on the neck. Her eyes fluttered closed and she exhaled in complete bliss at the touch of his lips on her skin and his presence by her side.

"Here I am. And where have you been?" Noelle questioned, her smile widening with each word.

"I was sharing a drink with your Pops and Dre, then Richie came over. It was a whole thing," Jackson replied, waving his hand in exasperation.

"Uh oh!."

"Nah, it was cool. I just can't drink with yo' Daddy. My damn chest still burning!"

Noelle laughed and soothingly rubbed her palm against the center of his chest. Jackson pulled her hand to his lips and kissed his way from her palm up to her fingertips, winking at her seductively. Noelle playfully blew a kiss at him and laced her fingers through his.

"To answer your question, Eric," Noelle started as she looked over at him. "I'm great!"

"Looks like it," Eric said flippantly.

"You enjoy the rest of your night, alright? *Al-right*!" Noelle said sarcastically as she walked away hand-in-hand with Jackson gleefully following behind her.

Jackson nodded his head and tipped his drink at Eric as they passed by. Eric followed the pair with his eyes as they disappeared onto the crowded dance floor. He wasn't lying when he said Noelle looked good. He always thought she was beautiful, but this time was different. The smooth, flawless cocoa skin of her face surrounded by lush golden-brown curls, the sensuous curves of her body and long sexy legs that he could never get enough of back in the day. Not much about her had changed, but the last five years had certainly been phenomenal to her, in his opinion.

Eric caught a subtle glimpse of her through the crowd, watching her hips and hair sway to the music. He could even still smell her perfume in the air around him.

"Eric!" a voice shouted from behind him.

He turned around to find an annoyed Marguerite standing there with her hands on her hips. For a moment he just stood there silently, staring into the glaring eyes of his fiancée – the woman he chose. With a heavy sigh, Eric gulped down the last of his drink, sat the empty glass on a nearby table and followed Marguerite as she led the way to her mother's table.

The DJ made an announcement that the New Year was thirty minutes away, and the waitstaff began circulating trays of champagne-filled flutes. On all the tables were confetti poppers for everyone to let off once the ball dropped. Noelle and Jackson were at the table with her parents, grandmother, siblings and their dates. The night had consisted of dancing, funny stories and flirty comments from her grandmother that were aimed at both Jackson and Aundre. All-in-all, it was shaping up to be everything Noelle could have possibly hoped for.

When the DJ started the ten minute countdown to midnight and put the digital numbers on the jumbo screen behind the booth for everyone to see, Jackson turned to his left and shared a knowing look with Aundre as they both watched the numbers tick down on the screen. They slapped hands and smiled. Jackson leaned over to Noelle and brushed the hair back from the side of her face as she was talking to her mom. At the feel of his hands on her, she turned to look at him and smiled instantly as she caressed his bearded face. He jerked his head to the right signaling for her to come with him, and she did so gladly.

The pair got up and walked towards the center of the room where a crowd was starting to gather for the final countdown. Jackson took hold of both Noelle's hands and pulled her close until they were toe-to-toe. Looking in her eyes at that moment made everything else around him disappear. All noise faded away and every other face in the crowd blurred out of sight.

"Baby," Jackson started, still holding her hands. "I don't want this year to end without you knowing that I am beyond in love with you."

Noelle's smile widened and she could feel tears welling up in her eyes. She leaned forward and kissed him happily on the lips.

"I love you, too," Noelle said breathily against his lips.

"Babe, from day one, every part of our love story has been so completely random and unexpected," Jackson continued. "I never thought that one day of just doing my job would lead to my whole world changing. I had been searching for you my whole life and didn't even know it. Honestly, I'd lost hope that you even existed, but I'm so thankful that I was wrong."

Jackson took a step back and lowered himself down until he was on one knee, still holding her left hand. Noelle gasped and covered her mouth with her free hand, trying to muffle her screams.

"Noelle Angelique Morgan, love of my life and answer to my every prayer. Will you marry me?"

Noelle rapidly nodded her "Yes," because she couldn't get her words past the lump forming in her throat. A huge grin spread across Jackson's face at her answer. He retrieved a black velvet box out of his pants pocket and opened it, revealing a two carat emerald cut diamond engagement ring. The stone sparkled and flickered more than the strobe lights in the party.

As Jackson slid the ring on her finger, they could hear everyone shouting "Happy New Year!" He stood up, grabbed her face in his hands and said "Happy New Year, Baby," then kissed her tenderly under a confetti rain shower.

Fifteen

"I'll never get tired of looking at this rock on your finger!" Debra squealed as she held up Noelle's hand to admire the engagement ring Jackson had given her three weeks ago.

The diamonds flickered and danced under the salon lights. Every day since Jackson proposed to Noelle, when she'd walk into work Debra would ask to see the ring and her excited squeal was always the same.

"And I'll never get tired of showing it off!" Noelle chirped with glee as she wiggled her fingers.

"I'm so happy for you, Sis," Debra said, still smiling down at the ring. "So, when do we start planning?"

"Girl! Can I enjoy the engagement part first?!" Noelle exclaimed as she snatched her hand away from Debra.

"I mean, yeah of course. But, also hurry up!" Debra shouted back with a laugh.

"Anyway," Noelle said with a smack of her lips. "Is everything set up and ready to go in the spa loft?"

"Yes, ma'am. Time slots are all blocked off and the techs are all ready for you."

"Perfect!"

Noelle had reconciled with most of her family after the New Year's Eve party and New Year's Day brunch at her parents' house that followed. She decided that life was better lived surrounded by those she loves and who she knows loves her. Noelle was determined to keep Nani Ester's words of wisdom from Christmas close to her heart when it came to her family, and today was another step in that direction.

Noelle blocked off three hours and invited her mom, Annabelle, her grandmother Ernestine, her Aunt Carolyn and few other extended relatives to come to the salon for a small spa day, complete with facials and mani-pedis. This was something she used to do at least once a month with her mom, granny and sister a few years ago, but since Shandra had gone away to college, Noelle hadn't done them as often. It probably also had a lot to do with Shandra threatening to "Knock all this shit over!" if they continued the spa days without her. But, today she was willing to make an exception and just attend virtually.

Even though Noelle had no intentions of actually attending Marguerite's wedding this weekend, she knew many ladies in her family were going. So, she offered up the spa day as a way to just hang out together, and to also help them get primped and prepped for the weekend festivities. After all, her real beef was with Marguerite and Aunt Gladys, who she purposely hadn't invited.

Noelle was looking over her schedule for the next few days with Debra when the salon door chimed and the face of her mother appeared. With huge smiles spread across their faces, Annabelle and Noelle rushed into each others' arms and hugged tightly. They giggled with excitement and rocked side-to-side as their arms got tighter and tighter.

"Oh, she the only damn person you see? Gimme some of that!" Ernestine fussed behind Annabelle.

"I'm sorry, Granny. Come here!" Noelle said, pulling her in for the same tight hug.

Noelle greeted each of her guests as they filed into the salon for their

4PM appointment. Debra escorted the group upstairs to the spa loft that had been decorated in white and rose gold. All of the pedicure chairs were draped in rose gold satin chair covers and the side tables next to each chair held a champagne flute, plate of chocolate covered strawberries and a single white rose.

Each of the manicure stations had white plastic tablecloths over them with gold and rose gold confetti lightly sprinkled over the top. Noelle had written "Welcome, Lovelies" in calligraphy using a white paint marker on the mirror wall so the ladies would see it as soon as they made it to the top of the stairs. The soothing sounds of Anita Baker crooning from the speakers and the smell of lavender and jasmine candles filled the air. The ambiance was definitely set.

"Ladies, welcome to your Spa Day Escape," Noelle announced once they were all in the loft. "Today is all about you. We will cater to your every need and make you feel even better than you did before you got here. We have facials and waxes going on to your left, and nails to the right. Manicures, pedicures and even hand massages. We have chilled champagne waiting and some pineapple juice if you'd like to make a mimosa. You ask and we shall provide. Enjoy!"

The next few hours passed by in a hail of laughter, clinking glasses and impromptu karaoke as Noelle and her staff catered to her family. They even indulged in some light rowdy and raunchy conversations, some of which even made Noelle blush. Her grandmother was in the middle of recalling the racy details of a story involving Noelle's grandfather, the backseat of an old school Cadillac and some Sam Cooke when Shandra called on Google Meets.

"Thank God!" everyone shouted, cutting off Granny's story.

Noelle answered from her phone and projected the video call onto one of the flat screen TVs suspended from the ceiling and used her Bluetooth speaker for sound. That way everyone could see and speak to Shandra while she attended the spa day virtually. She was in her dorm room with a clay facemask on and painting her toes. Noelle smiled at the sight of her sister on the screen and the women around her and was so grateful to have moments like this once again.

The strong stench of a cognac flavored cigar mingled with the night air as Eric Pastor sat by the cobblestone firepit on his patio. He was deep in thought and nursing a glass of Jameson. There was a bit of a chill in the air as the breeze brushed against the back of his neck. The crickets and crackling wood played a nighttime symphony around him. It was the same tonight as it had been every night since the New Year's Eve party. A stiff drink, a lit cigar and cold air to help numb the stinging of his wounded pride.

The moment Eric spotted Noelle and Jackson walking arm-in-arm across the hotel parking lot, he'd felt this ache he couldn't explain. Him having any feelings whatsoever surrounding Noelle Morgan at this point made no sense. It felt like a lifetime had passed since their marriage ended, and obviously, he had moved on. But, to see her doing the same with his own two eyes burned more than the Irish whiskey sliding down his throat.

It was the way her eyes lit up when she heard his voice. The smile that formed at the sight of his face. How the tension in her shoulders and forehead immediately released. The way her body nearly melted into him the moment he touched her. Or maybe it was the smug assuredness on Jackson's face as they walked away. Honestly, all of it made Eric sick to his stomach.

Perhaps it's just his mind playing tricks on him. Just last minute jitters before the big day on Saturday. Even though it's his second stroll down the aisle, Eric admittedly felt a little nervous as the minutes, hours and days ticked by to his wedding day approaching. *Yeah, that's it. Just nerves getting to me. Nothing more*, he thought to himself.

"You plan on staying out here all night," a voice broke through the silence from behind him. "Or are you coming in to help finalize this seating chart with me and *your mama*?"

Eric let out a heavy sigh and downed his drink in one swift gulp. The stinging in his throat made him wince a little, but it didn't stop him from refilling his cup to the rim. Eric stood and turned to see his fiancée, Marguerite, glaring at him from the patio door with her hands on her hips.

He had stepped outside to grab a quick smoke, but that turned into an hour and a half long smoke and ponder session. Eric had a lot on his mind and just needed a moment to himself. Probably would've been better to pick a moment that didn't result in leaving his mother, Rose, and Marguerite alone, though. To say they couldn't stand each other, was putting it mildly. It may have been because Eric's mother wasn't shy about expressing her true feelings towards "that gal," as she often called her.

Mama Rosie would tell anyone with two ears just how much she loved and favored Noelle, her "forever daughter-in-law," and just how disappointed she was in Eric for, "Messing that up!"

"Of all the fool ass things to do!" Mama Rosie would often yell with little to no prompting.

Even though her doing so would agitate Eric to no end, lately he found himself almost agreeing with his mother. For years, he rationalized that he and Noelle just weren't as meant to be as they had once believed and it was only a matter of time before it all went up in flames anyway. But maybe not. Maybe...

"Eric!" Marguerite broke through the silence once more.

Eric stared at his fiancée – his very soon-to-be wife – and blinked slowly, not saying a word. He just exhaled another heavy sigh, took a long drink of his Jameson – nearly emptying the glass again – shrugged his shoulders and made his way towards the door to go back inside. Eric took two steps before turning on his heels to grab the bottle of whiskey off the table to take inside with him.

"Definitely gonna need this," he mumbled as he walked towards a pissed off Marguerite.

◇ ◇ ◇ ◇ ◇ ◇

"Mama, what made you marry Daddy?" Noelle asked curiously.

She had gone to her parents house after closing up the salon for the night. After their Spa Day Escape, Noelle and her lady kin migrated to her parents house, much to Richard's chagrin. The gathering didn't last too long, because his unmasked annoyance started making some people uncomfortable. Not that he cared.

"Probably boredom," Annabelle said with a laugh.
"Ma!" Noelle exclaimed with a laugh of her own.
"What?! Ok, my bad," Annabelle snickered.
"That was a serious question, Ma'am!" Noelle chuckled.
"Oh. Well, besides being obnoxiously in love with his ol' surly self? I'd have to say it was because in all my life, I never felt like more of a woman *and* a lady than I did with him."
"Hmm, what do you mean?"
"Meaning, he made me feel sexy and appreciated and desired and

empowered and adored and wanted constantly. Feeding my woman-hood. And at the same time, he was so protective and supportive. A consummate gentleman. Even to this day, I never touch a door handle or pull out my own chair if I'm with him. I'm talking about his jacket over a puddle, kinda stuff. Treating me like a lady, at all times."

"Aww, look at Daddy!"

"Yeah, and even when we're at each other's throats, and you know how bad that can get."

"Yeah, I do."

"Even then, he's never mean or nasty or the least bit disrespectful. In thirty-five years, thirty-eight if we count our courtin' years, Richard has never laid a hand on me that wasn't lovin', or raised his voice for any other reason 'sides callin' my name from a distance. He said he never would because to do so would mean he didn't love me in that moment, and there is never a moment when Richard James Morgan, Sr. does not love me. His words, not mine."

Hearing her mother's words made Noelle smile wide. Throughout her life, she'd witnessed her parents' love in real-time. Her father was very attentive, gentle and even flirty with his wife practically all the time. Like Annabelle said, even when they were having spats, he still spoke in a tone coated with love and care while making his point. Richard also extended that same level of care to his children.

No matter how angry or disappointed he was with them in the moment, he never used his words as weapons. Because he took his duties as a husband and father very seriously, and they didn't go away just because he was upset. Love takes no days off where Richard Morgan was concerned.

"Did you ever have any doubts that y'all would make it?" Noelle asked.

"When he first enlisted in the army," Annabelle replied without hesitation.

"Really? Why? The long-distance thing?" Noelle asked.

"Because he tried to go without tellin' me."

"I'm sorry, what?!"

"Tuh!"

"Take it that didn't go well?"

"Not at all! I told him if he was gonna leave me, he was gonna have to look me in the eyes and say it to my face first."

"And how'd that go?"

"He said, 'How can I look you in the eyes while I'm rippin' my heart out my chest?' And girl, I was speechless! Then, he told me that he wasn't enlistin' to leave me, but to go secure a better future for himself, so when he came back he'd have more to offer me. I said if you couldn't just talk to me about all of this before even makin' a decision this big, then clearly we ain't doin' what I thought we were doin'. And I left him standin' right there on his granny's porch."

"So, how did y'all get through it?"

"He came to see me the day he was to leave. Like early as hell in the morning because his train was leavin' later that night. He came to my house and asked for the day. 'Just give me this day with you,' is what he said. And so I did. It was twelve of the most beautiful hours any girl could ask for. That day is really where our life together began."

Noelle listened intently as her mother spun and swooned over the tail of "Rich & Anna B," as they were affectionately known back in the day. Hearing other people's love stories was always one of Noelle's favorite things to do. It reaffirmed for her that love is always possible and it comes in a variety of circumstances, situations and lifestyles. Nothing and nobody was perfect, but to find the one who was perfect for you is what truly mattered most.

Richard and Annabelle fought for their relationship with everything they had and refused to let each other give up or take the easy way out, no matter what they were facing. He enlisted in the army and Annabelle went to the University of Texas-Houston, as she put it, "Just to make those four years go by faster." During his third year of service, Richard was able to come home on a three month leave, and decided to take full advantage.

The day he landed back in Houston, he went to Annabelle's parents to seek permission to marry their daughter, to which they happily obliged. Later on that evening, Richard proposed to the love of his life while sitting on the beach watching the Fourth of July fireworks. Two weeks later they were married and had a two month long honeymoon until it was time for him to return to base.

To have a man who was so seriously devoted to you that he'd let nothing stop him from being with you, was something Noelle had always dreamed of, and now looking down at the diamond ring adorning her finger, she knew she had found him. Her parents had truly set the bar for Black Love in Noelle's eyes, and unbeknownst to Jackson, he had reached it and was even well on his way to surpassing it.

Quietly, Noelle whispered, "Thank you, God."

Sixteen

Noelle swore she'd never heard the salon door chime so many times as it had today.

"I know it's Saturday, but geez," she had mumbled to herself in between clients.

She had one under the dryer, one at the sink getting shampooed and another in the chair at her station, who had just come from the sink to rinse out the excess color and was now ready for styling. Noelle was raking the comb attachment of the blow dryer through her client's hair when she heard the doors chime again. She let out an exasperated grunt.

Before she could turn around to see who it was, she heard Debra go, "Uh, nope! No, ma'am! You cannot be in here and you know that!" She was coming from around her desk to block Marguerite's path when she entered the salon.

Noelle's mouth dropped and then immediately snapped shut, pursing her lips and clenching her jaw. Instead of reacting, she stayed focused on the client in front of her and let Debra handle the light weight trash formerly known as her cousin.

"Noelle!" Marguerite shouted from the front of the salon as she shuffled back and forth trying to get around Debra.

"She's busy and *you* need to leave!" Debra exclaimed.

"I don't care! I need *her*! Noelle!" Marguerite shouted again.

"No, you need to leave."

"And you need to get out of my face!"

"Or?"

There was a momentary hush that fell over the room as everyone watched the heated exchange between Debra and Marguerite. The two ladies locked eyes and stood firmly, ready for whatever was to happen.

"*Or*?!" Debra repeated with angry emphasis and a raised eyebrow.

"Hey! Cut it out! This is a place of business!" Noelle shouted authoritatively from her station.

"Noelle...please," Marguerite now pleading with her voice cracking.

Noelle looked at Marguerite through narrowed eyes, skeptical of what she wanted or why she was there. Marguerite was quite maniacal, manipulative and vindictive, but she was never a crier. She thought tears showed weakness, and that's something she refused to ever do. So, for her to come to Noelle, of all people, with tears in her eyes in *public*, had to mean that something was really, very wrong. Noelle huffed and rolled her eyes in frustration.

"You got two minutes," Noelle groaned as she turned her attention back to her client's hair.

Marguerite pushed past Debra and practically ran to Noelle's side, who eyed her with pure disgust. Noelle looked down at her watch and then back at Marguerite to emphasize her seriousness about that two minutes.

"I...I need your help...please," Marguerite said tearfully.

"With?" Noelle replied dryly.

Marguerite slowly pulled off the scarf wrapped around her head to reveal her severely damaged hair. It looked like she had dyed it, but the color was blotchy and noticeably uneven. Whatever chemicals were used on her hair drastically stripped it of any moisture, leaving it dry and brittle, along with the discoloration. In a word, it was BAD.

"Wha-what the..." Noelle's voice trailed off as she ran her fingers through Marguerite's hair, inspecting the damage.

"I know!" Marguerite wailed as she buried her face in her hands.

"Girl, who did you go to and what did they do to you?!" Noelle asked as she turned Marguerite around to get a full view of her head.

"I went to my mother's stylist," Marguerite started. "She's been doing Mama's hair for years, and I did two test runs with her over the last few months just to make sure she knew what she was doing. So, yesterday I went in to get my color treatment with plans to go back this morning for my style and eyebrows. But when I woke up and saw my hair, I damn near fainted!"

Marguerite had always been a very vain young woman who prided herself on her looks, especially her hair. It was always long and thick, never being any shorter than up to her shoulders. It was naturally dark brown and full of body. But today, it was discolored and ashen nearly beyond recognition or repair. Almost all of its raw, lush exuberance was gone.

"I'm sorry that happened to you," Noelle said with a dismissive shrug.

"Noelle, please," Marguerite started, a noticeable tremble in her voice. "Ca-can you just for a minute...just forget that you know me. Forget our history and everything that's happened, and just simply look at me as a woman. I am a woman who looks like *this* on her *wedding day*."

At first, Noelle only offered up a silent, blank stare with a slow blink.

Then her eyes narrowed as if she were zeroing in on something. Her eyes surveyed Marguerite's destroyed tresses, then studied every inch of her face as if she were just seeing it for the first time. Finally, Noelle looked her cousin in the eyes – her gaze was piercing and invasive.

Then, she dragged her gaze away from Marguerite back to her client's head. Noelle began parting sections in the woman's hair and slid the metal barreled curling iron inside the ceramic stove to heat up, making a loud clanging sound. In all this time she never uttered a word.

"Was your hair going to be up or down?" Noelle finally asked, her tone still dry and emotionless.

"Down," Marguerite whispered, still choking back tears.

"Side part or middle part?"

"Uh...middle, I guess."

"Bangs or no bangs?"

"I, uh...hadn't thought about that"

"How is your veil attached? Clip, comb or tiara?"

"It's a convertible with a comb and tiara. I can use either one."

"I'm sure I know which one you'll go with."

Noelle grabbed a section of her client's hair, wrapping the strands around the barrel of the curling iron and clamping it close, letting the heat seep in, before twirling her wrists clockwise and releasing a steaming hot, bouncy curl. All the while, Noelle purposely ignored Marguerite's antsy, anxious heavy breathing and shuffling back and forth that she saw out of her peripheral view.

Just as Marguerite was about to give up and grunt about this all being a waste of time, Noelle spoke up again.

"Hey, Tiffy!" Noelle called out over her right shoulder.

"Ma'am?" Tiffany replied as she swept around her station, pretending not to be eavesdropping.

"I got a shampoo, a deep...*deep* conditioner and hot oil treatment. You got me?"

"Yes, Ma'am."

Noelle closed her eyes, took a deep breath, rolled her shoulders and cracked her neck all to ease the tension and shake off the desires of pettiness she felt deep in her bones. Then she looked over at Marguerite once again, dragging her gaze from her face down to her shoes and back up to face.

"Go," Noelle said flatly.

Marguerite covered her mouth with her hands to hold back her gleeful screams and cries of appreciation. She stepped towards Noelle, ready to pull her in for a big hug, but Noelle stopped her cold and said, "Aht! We don't do that. Go." Marguerite meekly whispered her thanks and rushed off to meet Tiffany at the sink.

"I ain't tryna be nosey or nothing," Noelle's client started. "But, that was nice of you. Considering it sounds like y'all don't really fool with each other."

"Eh, I'm just tryna get into heaven," Noelle replied jokingly.

The two women shared a laugh as Noelle completed curling her client's hair.

"Beautiful!" she exclaimed as she snatched the plastic cape off.

Noelle finished up her next two clients rather quickly and was ready to get started on Marguerite's hair. She told her to have a seat and that she'd be right back. Noelle went down the short hallway at the back of the salon leading to the supply closet. She grabbed six auburn Virgin Brazilian Body Wave Bundles out of a large tote bin on the floor and headed back to her station.

Marguerite was sitting in the chair with puffy eyes and a tear-dampened face that was almost as wet as her hair. For a brief second, Noelle felt bad for her. Of all the days to have a hair emergency, your wedding day had to be the absolute worst time. Noelle opted to put professionalism before revenge and make Marguerite look mind-blowingly beautiful today.

The second Marguerite felt Noelle fan the plastic cape over her body and press the Velcro closed against her neck, she became a puddle of tears. She cried so hard, her body trembled. Noelle gave Marguerite's shoulders a gentle, reassuring squeeze that made her calm down a little.

Noelle made it a point to turn the chair so it wouldn't be facing any mirrors, hoping that would ease Marguerite's current anxiety and in-security. They didn't talk much, which wasn't the norm for Noelle. She always liked playing catch up and gossiping with her clients, but she knew all she ever needed to know about Marguerite, and even that was too much.

"You can open your eyes now, " Noelle said softly as she fanned out the curled ends of Marguerite's hair around her shoulders.

Marguerite slowly opened her tear-weighted lids to see her reflection in the mirror. Noelle had given her a beautiful twenty inch auburn-hued sew-in with loose curls and subtle fringed bangs. All evidence if her previous hair crisis was completely hidden, and she couldn't be happier. As Noelle gently placed the tiara veil on Marguerite's head and neatly tucked the metal ends beneath her hair, Marguerite burst into tears again and her entire body shook as she succumbed to every ounce of emotion she felt.

Noelle gave Marguerite another comforting squeeze of her shoulders and pulled the plastic cape off. Marguerite stood up and took several deep breaths, trying to calm her nerves so she could speak. With tears still streaming, but feeling slightly calmer, she turned to face Noelle.

"Noelle, I am so sorry," Marguerite started.
"What?" Noelle asked, confusion all over her face.
"I've always been so jealous of you my whole life," Marguerite said, her voice cracking with every word. "You were everybody's favorite everything, and you were one of the nicest people in the world. Always so good to me, and all I ever was was terrible to you."
"Marguerite, you don't have to..."
"You were there for me when everybody else gave up on me, and I betrayed you in the worst way. I didn't even have the decency to stab you in the back. I looked you right in the eyes and drove that dagger into your heart. And for that, I am so goddamn sorry."

Noelle placed her hand on her heart and a tight knot of emotions formed in her throat as Marguerite's words sank in. This was a moment she never dreamed would come. She had spent years learning how to be okay with the apology she'd never get. But, here it was...*The Apology.*

Noelle held out her hands and Marguerite grabbed hold. They took two steps towards each other, their hands still locked together. Noelle pressed her forehead to Marguerite's and squeezed her hands, letting her know that all was well, all was good and all was forgiven. It signified that they were locked in to healing beyond what tried to break them.

Noelle softly took Marguerite's face in her hands and placed a loving kiss on her forehead, because in this moment she wasn't the woman who hurt her or broke up her marriage. Right now Marguerite was just her little cousin again – the little cousin she always loved like a sister.

"Come on, Baby Girl," Noelle whispered. "Let's get you married."

Just then Gladys walked through the salon's door. Noelle had texted her earlier letting her know what was going on and around what time Marguerite would be ready. The way Gladys cried at seeing that message was nothing compared to how she cried when she walked in the salon to see her only daughter and her favorite niece embracing each other. She longed and prayed for this day and now that it was here, the tears couldn't be stopped.

Noelle hugged her aunt and placed Marguerite's hand in Gladys's and said, "She's ready."

"Wow, Babe! That's major!" Jackson exclaimed.

Noelle had called him after wrapping up her last client of the day. She told him about what happened earlier when Marguerite came in, and how she had apologized for everything that happened between them over the years. Noelle felt renewed and freed up from all the negativity that had built a home for itself inside of her. The weight of anger, spitefulness and resentment had become too heavy for her to carry anymore and the minute Marguerite sat down in her chair, Noelle knew it was time to take that weight off and put it down.

"Yeah, it was time," Noelle said with a heavy sigh. "I needed to let that hurt go. She apologized, it felt very sincere and it was all I wanted for years. Just to have my pain and anguish be acknowledged and accounted for, and now it has been. I'm good now."

"That's great, Baby," Jackson said. "I'm happy for you. You definitely deserved an apology, and honestly from what you've told me about Marguerite, I gotta say I never expected it to come from her. Glad I was wrong."

"Honestly, I never did either, but here we are. Amends made and all is well."

They talked for a while more, catching each other up on the contents of their day. Jackson was on another three-day stretch of overnight shifts, so they hadn't seen much of each other, but they made time to talk every day.

"So, how much is it frowned upon to sneak your fiancée into the firehouse? Just curious," Noelle asked mischievously.

"Ha! Very much frowned upon, but I'm willing to risk it," Jackson said flirtatiously.

"I bet you are!" she replied with a laugh.

"I'm just saying! We got beds, showers, a full kitchen, and a 72-inch TV. I mean it's a very inviting environment."

"Are you trying to tempt me, Mr. Howard?"

"*Entice* is more the word I think you're looking for, Ms. Morgan."

"Oh, I see. Well, in that case..."

Before Noelle could finish her sentence, she heard a knock on the salon's front door. The shop was closed and everyone had left for the night, but she had stayed to clean up and do some last minute paperwork. The lights were still on, which is probably why whoever it was thought the shop was still open.

"Uh, Baby, somebody is knocking on the door. Let me call you back," Noelle groaned.

"You sure? It's after hours and you're alone. I can stay on the phone," Jackson urged.

"No, I'm okay, I promise. It won't take long."

"Okay. Don't make me pull up, because I will."

"Aww, I love you too, Baby."

Noelle hung up and walked out of her office towards the front of the salon. She saw what looked like a man's silhouette against the closed blinds on the door. For a second she got nervous and regretted not keeping Jackson on the phone, but took a deep breath and continued to the door. Noelle parted the blinds with her fingers and was startled by who she saw.

"Eric?" she asked through the closed door.

"Yeah...uh, hey, Nola," Eric stammered as he anxiously paced in front of the door.

"What are you doing here?" she asked nervously.

"I...uh...can...can we talk for a second?"

"Can we *what*?!"

"Talk. I need to talk to you. Now. Please."

"Don't you have somewhere you're supposed to be right now?!"

"Um, yeah. That's why I need to talk to you."

Noelle eyed Eric suspiciously through the blinds as she watched him pace back and forth in his black and white wedding tuxedo. He looked sweaty and disheveled, which was very unlike him. Eric was always well-groomed and put together. Never a hair out of place or without a freshly pressed suit. But, here he stood on her doorstep with his shirt untucked and sweat stained, bow tie undone and hanging loosely around his neck, and one of his leather oxfords were untied. Eric Pastor looked messy, unkempt and out of sorts. Something was definitely wrong.

"Are you okay?" Noelle asked with concern in voice.

"I, uh...I don't know," Eric said breathlessly as he stopped pacing and looked at her through the glass door.

There was something in Eric's eyes that created a nervous knot in Noelle's stomach. She didn't know what was wrong, but just like her cousin earlier, Noelle knew this wasn't the Eric she remembered. Something wasn't right and it was written all over his face. She took her fingers out of the blinds and stared at the closed door. She wrung her hands, trying to shake off the foreboding feeling rising up within her. *What the hell is up with this day*?! Noelle thought to herself as she cautiously unlocked the bolts on the door and creaked it open. The windchimes barely tinkled with how gingerly she opened the door.

Eric stepped across the threshold into the salon. He had heard about Noelle's salon for years from his mother, Mama Rosie, but had never seen it in person. Though, he was certain he probably was never supposed to, especially if Noelle had anything to do with it. Yet, here he was knocking and she let him in. Hopefully, that was a sign that this wasn't a wreckless fool's errand.

Once inside, Eric began anxiously pacing again. He kept letting out loud exhales almost like he was hyperventilating. Noelle watched his dizzying movements in silence for a few minutes before demanding a reasonable explanation as to why he was here and not at his wedding reception, where he belonged.

"That is the million dollar question, ain't it?" Eric huffed as he kept pacing.

"That you still haven't answered," Noelle replied, sounding annoyed.

"Marguerite told me," he said flatly as he shuffled and clacked loudly across the tiled floor.

"Told you what?" she asked with a raised brow.

"About how she came to you. How she apologized."

Eric stopped pacing and turned to face Noelle. *God, she's beautiful*, he thought. He wanted so badly to touch her again. To take her in his arms and just...

"Yeah, she did. Gotta say I was shocked but I really appreciated it," Noelle said as a smile started to appear.

Eric took two steps towards Noelle, just trying to close the gap between them. As he did, the smile on Noelle's face quickly disappeared and her eyes narrowed, asking more questions than her lips could form.

"It got me thinking about how I still owed you that, too," Eric went on. "I mean even during the divorce and all the fallout, I kept trying to give you all this materialistic stuff. Just everything I thought you deserved, because I figured it was the least I could do, but that's not what you wanted. What you wanted, what you truly deserved more than anything was an honest apology."

Eric took another step towards Noelle, bringing him close enough to grab her hand. He stroked the back of it with his thumb as he continued on.

"Noelle, you were a damn good woman. Better than I ever deserved, that's for sure. You were always there loving and supporting me so selflessly. Everything about you was just so...pure. Genuine. And I took that for granted. I took *you* for granted."

Noelle continued to watch Eric through squinted eyes, looking back and forth between his face and the hand holding hers. Every time she tried to pull her hand away, he tightened his grip – like he was holding on for dear life and never wanted to let go.

"Believe it or not, my biggest regret in life is hurting you," Eric continued. "In all my mistakes, missteps and failures in life, and trust me there have been plenty. What I did to you, to us, was the worst. A lifetime of knowing each other and I destroyed everything we had. Noelle, there aren't enough words to tell you how sorry I am for all of it."

Eric pulled Noelle close, pressing their bodies together. He cupped her face in his hands and lowered his mouth to hers. Just as their breaths met and lips touched, Noelle bit down hard on Eric's bottom lip, making him pull back and yelp in pain.

"What the hell?!" Eric shouted as he repeatedly touched his lip to check for blood.

"Are you doing?!" Noelle shouted back as if finishing his sentence. "Did you really think you could waltz in here on your *wedding day* with some johnny-come-lately half-ass apology and I was just gonna fall into your arms?!"

"No! No, that's not what I was..." Eric stammered.

"Yeah, it was! You just got married *to-day*! To my *cousin*! Who you cheated with while you were married to *me*! What kinda sick ass game of tug-o-war do you think this is?"

"Noelle, it's not like that."

"Oh, so what is it like, Eric?"

"I just..."

"You just what?!"

"Noelle, you are the love of my life. You always have been, and you always will be. I have never loved anyone...I *will* never love anyone the way I love you."

"God, I hope not."

Noelle brushed past Eric, angrily marching towards her office. He quickly stepped after her, grabbing her by the arm. Noelle spun on her heels, swatted his hand away and pushed him backwards. The rage and disgust was so present on her face it was frightening.

"What the hell is that supposed to mean?!" Eric asked, sounding offended.

"It means you spent two years of college and two years of marriage professing how much you love and adore me," Noelle barked. "And then you cheated on me in my house with my own blood and when I chose to leave, you chose to let me. You chose to stay in New York building a life with the other woman. *That* is how you loved me, Eric. I wouldn't wish that on any woman. Not even Marguerite. She doesn't deserve that and she doesn't deserve this, and you know it."

Noelle's words cut through Eric like a hot knife through butter, and stung just as much. He stood there in stunned silence staring at Noelle's angry face, letting her venomous words sink in. No matter how much they burned, he knew they were true.

"Noelle, I didn't come here to see you just so I could hurt her," Eric said softly.

"Maybe not, but you do know that if she knew you were here, that *would* hurt her," Noelle said with her arms folded.

"Look, I do love Marguerite. I do," he emphasized.

"Then love her better than you loved me," she said pointedly.

Eric let out a heavy sigh as he wiped his hands down his face in frustration. He had snuck out of his reception after claiming he felt sick and was just going outside to get some air. He got in his car and drove here, blindly guided by some incessant need and desire to be in Noelle's presence. Eric had no idea why or what he even expected to come from this visit, but this definitely wasn't how it went in his head.

As much as he hated to admit it, Noelle was right, and the longer Eric stood there the more wrong he felt. It was his wedding day. He'd literally said, "I do," to Marguerite mere hours ago, but here he was pleading with and professing feelings for his ex-wife. No, Marguerite was nowhere near angelic or perfect, but Eric knew she didn't deserve this kind of betrayal and pain. She came to Noelle to apologize so she could enter her own marriage with a clear conscience and clean slate, and now her new husband was here threatening to destroy it before it even got started.

"You're right," Eric huffed, feeling slightly ashamed. " I know I have no right to ask, but..."

"Stop," Noelle said, holding up her hand. "I won't tell her, because I find no joy in causing her pain. Just be better to her, Eric. Just do better."

Eric walked backwards two steps before turning on his heels to head towards the door. As he reached for the doorknob, he stopped to face her once again.

"Look, Noelle, I really am s..." Eric started but was cut off by Noelle shaking her head.

"Save it," Noelle said dryly. "Just knowing you have to live the rest of your life with the memory of this moment and how it feels, is enough for me. Now go."

Eric simply nodded his head, opened the door and walked out into the chilly night air. Nothing more needed to be said. Noelle slammed the door closed and hurriedly locked it. She pressed her back against the door and let out a sigh of relief. For somebody who wanted to avoid Eric and Marguerite's wedding at all costs, Noelle was forced to see both of them today in near full wedding attire. Though it didn't bother her as much as she thought it would, she still could've lived without any and all of it.

As Noelle pushed off the door and started walking back to her office, her cellphone rang. The vibration in her hand startled her at first, but when she saw Jackson's smiling face and name flash across the screen, a rush of excitement hit her.

"Hey, Baby," Noelle sang into the phone.
"You were taking too long," Jackson said pointedly.
"Good lord!" Noelle huffed.
"I said it," Jackson said plainly.
"I feel so loved," she said sarcastically.
"I do love you. Ridiculously," he said sweetly.
"I know. I love you too."
"So what was taking so long? A last minute client?"

Noelle paused for a second, mulling over his question. Unlike Eric, she wanted her next marriage to be built on a solid foundation of truth and transparency, and that wasn't going to change today.

"No, actually it's a crazy ass story," she began.

Epilogue

Valentine's Day

"Shh, baby you gotta be quiet," Jackson whispered against Noelle's mouth.

They had snuck into one of the shower stalls at the firehouse for a quickie. Cradled in his arms with her legs wrapped around his waist and back pressed against the steam-covered wall, Noelle's body was shaking from her third orgasm and Jackson was trying to cover her screams. She bit down hard on her bottom lip and dug her nails into his shoulders with every deep thrust she felt. Jackson buried his face in her neck in an attempt to muffle his own moans as he gripped her hips.

They heard the door to the shower room open and they froze, while looking at each other and trying not to laugh. Another shower a few stalls over turned on and Noelle almost lost it. Jackson lowered her to the floor as he fought to contain his own snickering.

"Okay, we gotta go," Jackson whispered, gesturing with his thumb. "Hmm, one second," Noelle whispered back.

She pushed him against the wall and stood on her tiptoes to kiss him. The kiss was hungry, sensuous and full of more heat than their steaming shower. Noelle trailed her lips down his body before dropping to her knees and taking him into her warm mouth. Jackson tried to mask his shocked moan with a cough as he felt her lips wrap around him. Noelle dragged her lips excruciatingly slow from his base to tip, swirling her tongue along every inch. Jackson bit down on his fist, trying to muzzle his tortured groans.

The way Noelle unabashedly devoured him – holding his hips steady while her head bobbed and swiveled – made Jackson's knees weak. He gripped at the slippery walls trying to hold on while his body went through sexual agony. He felt his release coming on soon and it was getting harder for him to stay quiet now.

"Baby, I'm about to lose it," Jackson said breathlessly.

Noelle tightened her jaws, increasing the pressure as she sucked harder on him. Jackson dug his fingers into her scalp, grabbing handfuls of her hair as he got closer to going over the edge. His whole body jerked and twitched as he became more sensitive, telling Noelle that he was even closer to coming now. Then she released him from her mouth with a loud pop of her lips.

Noelle looked at Jackson and gave a mischievous smirk and wink before standing up. She kissed his chest, said, "Hold that thought. See you tonight," and slipped out of the shower, grabbing a towel off the bench on her way out. Leaving a shocked Jackson teetering on the edge of ecstasy with no release.

◇◇◇◇◇

"Why is your hair all wet?" Shandra asked when Noelle walked in the house.
"Oh, uh, no reason," Noelle said hurriedly.
"Liar! Whatchu do? Or better yet, *who* did you do?" Shandra asked with a smirk.

Noelle stuck out her tongue and laughed as she darted past her sister and headed up the stairs. Shandra had come to town to be with Aundre for their first Valentine's Day, and Noelle thought it would be fun to do a double date night since it was hers and Jackson's, too. Which was one of the reasons for that sneaky shower rendezvous at the firehouse.

Shandra burst into Noelle's room while she was in the closet looking for an outfit for the night.

"Don't you dodge my questions, Woman!" Shandra shouted when she came into the room.

"Not dodging. Just ignoring," Noelle said flippantly as she held up a burgundy dress.

"Same thing! And I'm wearing that one," Shandra said with a smirk.

Noelle cut her eyes at her sister and shook her head before slamming the hanger down on the rod. She forcefully raked more hangers across the rod until she found a champagne colored, backout dress and skeptically looked over at Shandra who held her hands up in surrender.

"You're gonna look hot!" Shandra complimented.

"Thanks. So will you," Noelle said with a half smile.

"Ew, don't be like that! Trust me, Jackson will love it," Shandra said with excitement.

"Right?!" Noelle squealed.

Shandra grabbed the burgundy one sleeve, asymmetrical dress out of the closet and hip bumped Noelle before skipping out of the room and sang, "You're not gonna look better than me, though!" Noelle laughed and shook her head at her sister, then went back to her closet to pick out shoes. Once their date night outfits were secured, both ladies hopped in the shower to finish primping and prepping before their beaus arrived.

Noelle was standing at the sink wrapped in her plush bath towel cleansing her face when she heard the chime of her cellphone letting her know she had a new text message. Before she could check it, she heard Shandra shout "Aww, what the fuck?!" from the guest bathroom in the hall. Noelle walked out of the master bathroom across her bedroom and stopped in the doorway when she saw Shandra standing in the hall.

"Did you get this text?" Shandra asked, sounding annoyed.

"I heard that I got a text, but I haven't checked my phone yet. What's wrong?" Noelle asked, sounding concerned.

"Dre just texted me that a call came in at the firehouse and they gotta go," Shandra said.

"Ugh! The cost of loving a first responder, I guess," Noelle said dejectedly.

"Bump that! I want my Valentine's Day, dammit!" Shandra exclaimed, stomping her feet.

"I know. Me too, but it's okay. As soon as that truck pulls up to the station, we're snatching them up!" Noelle said pointedly.

"Damn right!" Shandra concurred.

"But in the meantime, ice cream and binge watching!" Noelle exclaimed.

Shandra clapped her hands cheerfully before disappearing into the guest room to get dressed and Noelle did the same in her own room. They both threw on oversized sweatshirts, that happened to be Houston FD shirts they swiped from their boyfriends, and some leggings and footie socks. They gleefully trotted downstairs to veg out on the sofa until they heard back from Jackson and Aundre.

Noelle went to the kitchen to grab a carton of Breyers vanilla bean ice cream, spoons and two bottles of water before joining Shandra on the sofa. She was wrapped in a fleece blanket searching through the Netflix library for something to watch. Noelle plopped down next to her, popped the top on the ice cream and dug in, grateful for the chance to relax before date night.

◇◇◇◇◇◇

The mixture of end credits music blaring from the television and loud knocks at the front door startled Noelle awake. She and Shandra had fallen asleep while watching a movie and waiting for Jackson or Aundre to reach out to them. Noelle checked her cellphone for the time

and saw no missed calls or new texts from Jackson, but then just
assumed that was him knocking on the door. Nearly four hours had
passed since she had last heard from him and she was positive dinner
plans were canceled for the night. *He better have a damn good plan B*, she
thought.

Another series of loud knocks broke through Noelle's thoughts and
she got up to answer the door. Assuming it was who they were expecting, she just opened the door, but who she saw standing on the porch
caught her by surprise. It was Aaron Deckland, the Fire Chief from
Jackson and Aundre's station.

"Chief Deckland?" Noelle asked, sounding shocked and confused.
"Hey, Noelle. Sorry it's so late," Chief apologized.
"It's okay. Just surprised to see you, that's all."
"Yeah I get it. Would you mind if I…"
"Of course! Sorry! Please come in."

Noelle unlocked the glass paned screen door and pushed it open so
Chief Deckland could step inside. By now, Shandra had awakened and
was stretching on the sofa, but sat straight up when she saw the Chief.
They exchanged pleasantries, but his unexpected presence added a huge
air of confusion.

"I'm assuming the fire you guys got dispatched to is taken care of
now?" Shandra asked as she checked her own phone for missed calls or
messages.
"Uh, yeah. Yeah, it is. That's actually why I'm here," Chief Deckland
said sheepishly. "When it comes to my guys, I make it a point to get close
to their families and treat them how I'd want someone to treat mine."

Chief Deckland was pacing back and forth in the living room as he
spoke. Noelle leaned her back against the front door and folded her arms
as she hung on his every word. Shandra was anxiously perched on the
edge of the sofa with her forearms resting on her thighs and her hands
clasped together.

"I didn't want this to just be a phone call," Chief Deckland continued.

"You didn't want *what* to just be a phone call?" Shandra asked, her brows lifted.

He stopped pacing and looked into Shandra's waiting eyes, then he looked over at Noelle, whose eyes were full of worry. He exhaled a heavy sigh before he spoke again.

"There was an accident," Chief Deckland said softly, his voice cracking.

"What?!" Noelle and Shandra exclaimed in high pitched voices.

"Jackson and Aundre got caught inside and got hurt. It was bad," Chief went on. "We were able to get them out, but it's *bad*."

"Oh, my God!" Noelle said tearfully with her hands on her mouth.

"Where are they?" Shandra demanded as she grabbed her shoes and phone.

Noelle followed suit, putting on a pair of boots she had by the door and went to the closet to grab a jacket. She began frantically looking for her wallet and car keys while trying to keep her tears at bay. She found her keys on the kitchen counter and rushed back into the living room to find Shandra shouting at the Chief asking him what happened.

"Shandy, we're not sure yet, but..." he started but was cut off by Shandra's continued shouts.

"You were with them! How the hell do you not know?!" she exclaimed.

"Where are they, Chief? Tell me you at least know that?" Noelle interjected, her hands shaking so hard her keys jingled.

"Yeah, that I know," he replied.

"Okay, tell us where. Now." Noelle said.

"No offense, ladies, but neither of you should be driving right now. I'm heading over to the hospital. You can ride with me." Chief offered

"Good. Let's go." Shandra said as she snatched the front door open and headed outside to the Chief's truck.

<u>Until next time...</u>

ShaRhonda is originally from Maywood, IL, and currently resides in Metro Atlanta, GA. She is a self-proclaimed "Unhinged Creative," as well as owner and operator of S.L.S. Publishing, LLC. She has been published multiple times across various indie publications, including three self-published collections of poetry and a host of other projects.

ShaRhonda holds a Master's Degree from National Louis University in Chicago, and currently works a "cushy 9-5" as a means to fund the dream of being a best-selling author some day.

In between her many passion projects, she moonlights as a freelancer, content creator, copy writer and editor, and avid reader of fiction and poetry.

Follow along on her writing journey & check out her merch brand:
The S-L-S Collection